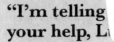

"I'm telling
your help, L

Conveniently Wed!

Conveniently wedded, passionately bedded!

Whether there's a debt to be paid, a will to be obeyed or a business to be saved...she's got no choice but to say, "I do!"

But these billionaire bridegrooms have got another think coming if they imagine marriage will be that easy...

Soon their convenient brides become the objects of inconvenient desire!

Find out what happens after the vows in:

Look for more Conveniently Wed! stories coming soon!

Sharon Kendrick

HIS CONTRACT
CHRISTMAS BRIDE

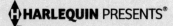 **HARLEQUIN** PRESENTS®

Recycling programs
for this product may
not exist in your area.

ISBN-13: 978-1-335-53876-5

His Contract Christmas Bride

First North American publication 2019

Copyright © 2019 by Sharon Kendrick

Printed in U.S.A.

Sharon Kendrick once won a national writing competition by describing her ideal date: being flown to an exotic island by a gorgeous and powerful man. Little did she realize that she'd just wandered into her dream job! Today she writes for Harlequin, and her books feature often stubborn but always *to-die-for* heroes and the women who bring them to their knees. She believes that the best books are those you never want to end. Just like life...

Books by Sharon Kendrick

Harlequin Presents

The Italian's Christmas Housekeeper

Conveniently Wed!

Bound to the Sicilian's Bed
The Greek's Bought Bride

One Night With Consequences

The Pregnant Kavakos Bride
The Italian's Christmas Secret
Crowned for the Sheikh's Baby

Secret Heirs of Billionaires

The Sheikh's Secret Baby

The Legendary Argentinian Billionaires

Bought Bride for the Argentinian
The Argentinian's Baby of Scandal

Visit the Author Profile page
at Harlequin.com for more titles.

This is for the magnificent Joan Bolland, whose wisdom and wry sense of humor are greatly appreciated. Xxx

PROLOGUE

DRAKON KONSTANTINOU LOOKED around him, unable to hide the disgust which swamped his body like a dank, dark tide. But hot on the heels of disgust came regret, and then guilt. Regret that he couldn't have done something sooner and guilt that he couldn't have prevented this terrible outcome.

But the trigger to these grisly events had been pulled a long time ago and he couldn't control everything, no matter how much he had spent his whole life trying to do just that. Sometimes control just slipped beyond your grasp and there was nothing you could do about it. His brother had gone now and so had the woman he'd married—the sordid paraphernalia strewn around the room the last testimony to their degenerate lifestyle.

But life went on.

Life *had* to go on.

As if to confirm that indisputable fact, he heard an unfamiliar cry coming from an adjoining room, quickly followed by a voice and the sound of footsteps.

'Drakon?'

He glanced up at his business partner's face as she walked in from the adjoining room. Gingerly, she walked towards him, clearly uncomfortable as she carried her precious cargo—as if unsure just what to do next. *Join the club,* thought Drakon grimly.

'Are you ready, Drakon?' she asked.

He wanted to shake his head. To tell her he wasn't prepared for this latest responsibility which had come slamming at him like a weighted curve ball. To protest that he'd done enough of shouldering other people's burdens and their problems and he needed a break. But that was impossible. He could do this. He *would* do this. He just hadn't quite worked out how.

He needed a woman, that was for sure, but a quick flick through his memory bank of females who would be willing to do pretty much anything he asked of them failed to come up with anyone remotely suitable.

And then, as if in answer to the turmoil of his thoughts, a face unexpectedly swam into his mind. A face with soft blue eyes the colour of the bluebells which had grown beneath the trees in those long-ago English springs, in the heady days before he'd discovered how much his father liked hookers.

Forcing his mind back to the present, he thought about the face again. Not a beautiful face but a kindly one. He felt a faint beat of remembered desire, but far stronger still was his sudden sense of purpose as he allowed his mind to linger on Lucy Phillips for the first time in many months and his eyes narrowed speculatively. Maybe fate was cleverer than he'd imagined. Maybe the answer had been staring him in the face all this time.

'Neh,' he said, his harsh Greek accent echoing around the marble-floored villa. 'I'm ready.'

CHAPTER ONE

AT FIRST SHE didn't recognise him, which was pretty amazing when she stopped to think about it. Except that Lucy had done her best *not* to think about it. Or him. She'd tried to blot Drakon Konstantinou from her mind, the way you did when you were on a diet and didn't want to focus on cream cake, or chocolate, or toasted teacakes swimming with melted butter.

Because only an idiot would want to remember the man who had introduced them to pleasure then walked away so fast his feet had barely touched the ground. Or to recall her own participation in what could only ever have been an impossible fantasy.

But it *was* him. Lucy's heart slammed against her ribcage as she opened the front door of her tiny cottage and peered out through the protective chain at the figure standing on the step, silhouetted darkly against the fiery orange of the winter sunset. It was definitely him. And the first thing she thought was how different he seemed from the man who had seduced her on the beautiful Greek island of Prasinisos, an island which he actually *owned*.

It wasn't just that his features were ravaged and his shoulders hunched, as if a heavy weight were pressing down on their muscular breadth, but his black hair was longer, too. Instead of being neatly clipped to follow the shape of his head, ebony waves were kissing the collar of his dark overcoat and there was a dark layer of stubble at his angled jaw. His appearance hinted more at recent neglect rather than his usual pristine perfection and it was an astonishing transformation. Suddenly Drakon Konstantinou bore more resemblance to a rock singer who'd spent the night on the tiles, rather than a powerful oil baron and shipping magnate, with the world at his fingertips.

Unwanted feelings flooded through her body and started making her skin feel as raw as if someone had been attacking it with a cheese grater. She told herself she shouldn't be so sensitive. Wasn't that what her former colleagues at the hospital used to tease her about? But sensitivity wasn't something you could just turn on and off, like a tap. Her memories of Drakon were mixed and...*complex*...and the overriding feeling she'd been left with when he'd walked away was that it would be better if she never saw him again. Better for her, certainly. Better to forget those three blissful days and nights which she suspected had ruined her for all other men. To try to get back into the groove of a life which had seemed very dull after her brief glimpse into *his* world.

But he was here now. Standing in front of her with all that dark, brooding power and she could hardly ignore him. She couldn't really shut the door in his face and tell him she was busy—something which her scruffy jeans and swimming club sweatshirt suggested was untrue. Because that would run the risk of making her look vulnerable and that was something she wasn't prepared to do. Okay, so he had taken her virginity. No, Lucy corrected herself sternly. She had *given* him her virginity—with an eagerness which had taken her completely by surprise. And him, if the look on his face had been anything to go by when he'd thrust deep into her body, while, outside, the inky waters of the Mediterranean had gleamed silver in the moonlight.

Just because they'd shared a passionate few days together and it had fizzled out like a spent firework didn't mean they should now be enemies. Or was she deluded enough to have expected that the amazing sex they'd shared would end in some sort of *relationship*, when they came from completely different worlds?

And yet...

She cleared her throat, trying to quell the foolish hope which was spiralling up inside her, knowing how foolishly persistent hope could be. False hope could raise you up and then dash you down again, making the pain even more intense than it had been before. And she was done with pain for the time being. Hadn't she been given more than her fair share of it during her twenty-eight years?

So she forced as wide a smile as she could manage and when she spoke, her breath rushed from her mouth like billowing smoke as it hit the cold winter air. 'Drakon,' she said. 'This is...unexpected.'

He shrugged his powerful shoulders. 'Maybe I should have rung first.'

He said it as if he didn't really mean it. As

if any woman should be falling over herself with gratitude that the famous Greek billionaire had deigned to pay her an unexpected call. She wasn't really feeling it but Lucy attempted indignation. 'Yes, you should. You were lucky I was in.'

Dark eyebrows were raised. 'Oh?'

And despite everything, she found herself offering an explanation. As if she needed to prove herself to a man who hadn't even cared enough about her to lift up the phone and check she was okay after their long weekend together. She began to talk. 'Because this is a busy time of year in the catering industry. There are a lot of pre-holiday functions coming up and normally I would be working. In case you don't remember I work for Caro's Canapés and people eat more canapés at Christmas than at any other time of the year.'

'Of course. Christmas.' Drakon tensed as he said it, knowing he needed to choose his words with care—not a normal occurrence for him, since people always hung onto whatever he had to say with an eagerness which sometimes repulsed him. Like many powerful men he demanded servility while secretly despising it, but Lucy was different. She had always been different. Wasn't that one of the

reasons he was here today? There were countless women who would have bitten his hand
off to accept what he was about to offer—but
only Lucy would understand the truth.

*Only Lucy would accept the limitations of
what he was about to ask her.*

But first he needed to gain entry into her
mini-fortress of a cottage. He fixed his gaze
on the chain which was still stretched tautly
across the door and wondered why she hadn't
released it.

'Can I come in?' he questioned.

There was a pause. Not long enough to
be insulting, but a pause nonetheless and he
noted it with surprise and a faint flicker of
irritation he knew to be unreasonable.

'I suppose so,' she said at last.

He watched her fiddle with the chain before pulling the door open and stepping back
to let him in. He noted that she was keeping
her distance but maybe he couldn't blame her
for that. He hadn't behaved particularly well
after that surprisingly erotic encounter which
had taken place back in the summer and afterwards he'd cursed himself for allowing it to
happen in the first place. He couldn't understand why he'd behaved in a way which had
been so uncharacteristic, because usually he

chose his lovers as carefully as he chose his cars—and normally someone like Lucy Phillips wouldn't have even made the cut.

He hadn't rung her or asked to see her again, because what was the point of meaningless phone calls which might have left her fabricating unfulfillable dreams about the future? She was way too unworldly to spend any time with a hard-hearted bastard like him. Not for the first time he found himself wondering what had possessed him to invite someone he'd known from his schooldays to his Greek island home, though deep down he knew why. It hadn't been because of the way she had looked at him with those soft blue eyes, nor the way she had blushed when she'd seen him again after so many years. It hadn't even been about her somewhat old-fashioned attitude, which had been obvious in pretty much everything about her—from the way she wore her hair to the polite way she'd tried to refuse his offer of a lift home after the reunion, saying it would take him miles out of his way—an attitude which had undoubtedly charmed him.

He'd done it because he'd felt sorry for her because she was hard-working and poor and had been through a tough time. And yet, against all the odds, he had seduced her, even though she was nothing like his usual choice of bed partner. He was not and never had been a player, for reasons which were rooted deeply in his past. In fact, if anything, he'd been described as not just formidable but indifferent to the charms of women. He was not indifferent, of course. Far from it. He loved sex as much as any red-blooded man but it took more than physical attraction to engage his interest. Throughout his life he'd been able to have his pick of any woman he wanted, but he was much too fastidious for that. When he did engage in a relationship, he liked women who were experienced. Sexual equals who were willing to experiment. Intelligent women more focussed on their career than on the idea of marriage, who treated sex like an enjoyable form of exercise. Not someone soft and gentle and full of wonder, like Lucy Phillips.

As she closed the door on the freezing winter afternoon, he was able to study her. Nobody in the world could ever have described her as pretty, although her soft brown hair was shiny and her skin was clear, and she had a way of looking at you with that misty

blue gaze which was more than a little unsettling…

He narrowed his eyes. And, yes, she had
a body made firm by youth and exercise but
the grey jeans she was wearing did her curvy
derrière no favours. Neither did her sweatshirt, which was scarlet and had the insig-
nia of a dolphin embroidered just below one
shoulder and disguised the luscious curve of
breasts he knew lay beneath. Suddenly he
couldn't hold back the flashback memory of
her nipples—rose-tipped and tasting of co-
conut sunscreen—which had been positioned
so tantalisingly beneath his questing lips as
he had licked them into cresting peaks. He
felt the hard rush of blood to his groin and
thought just how much he would like to lose
himself in her again.

*Until a rush of shame made him wonder
why the hell he was thinking about sex at a
time like this.*

Ever-present guilt washed over him and
Drakon shook his head to clear it. Focus, he
told himself fiercely. Focus. Think about the
reason you're here. The only reason you're
here. He looked around, realising that the
cramped dimensions and obvious lack of investment in the property she had inherited

from her mother was playing right into his hands. But before he put his proposition to her, he had to get her to relax and to lose that tight look from her face. Which wasn't going to be easy, judging from the way she was staring at him as warily as if a snake had just wriggled its way from the nearby river-bank into her tiny sitting room.

Stepping over the row of shoes lined up neatly beside the front door, he glanced around, at a jug of holly on a table and the way the scarlet berries echoed the colourful flash of cushions which were scattered along the sofa. A flickering fire was burning in the grate—scenting the small room with apple-wood. Everything was polished and shining and all the contents of the room seemed old and lovingly preserved. In pride of place on the wall were two photographs of differ-ent men, both in uniform, and Drakon felt a clench of pain and an unwanted sense of iden-tification. But he forced himself to concen-trate on the positive. On the future, not the past. Because that was what was important, he reminded himself fiercely. The only thing which was important.

'Nice place,' he commented, making the

kind of benign social observation which wasn't usually part of his vocabulary.

Her blue eyes narrowed suspiciously, as if she didn't believe him. As if he was secretly making fun of her by comparing this match-box of a dwelling to the sprawling square footage of his many homes. But he *did* mean it. He'd never been inside this riverside cottage before but he'd passed it often enough when he was rowing for the prestigious English boarding school he'd attended, where Lucy's mother had been matron. The little house used to symbolise home for all the boys who were so far away from their own. He remembered seeing fairy lights in the window and a wreath on the door every Christmas. He remembered hearing laughter coming through an open door in the lush months of summer when the green reeds grew tall and the riverbank was bosky. But there was no Christmas wreath today, he noted.

'It suits my needs perfectly,' she said, rather primly.

Her words sounded defensive and Drakon found himself staring at her left hand, registering each ringless finger before lifting his gaze to her eyes. It was unlikely that her situation had changed since the summer but you never knew... 'You live here alone?'

A faint frown appeared on her brow. 'I do.'

'So...there's no man in your life?'

Hot colour rushed into her cheeks. 'I believe that's what's known as a rather impertinent question.'

'Is there?' he persisted.

Her blush deepened. 'No. Actually, there isn't. Not that it's any of your business,' she said crossly, before fixing him with an enquiring look. 'Look, what can I do for you, Drakon? You turn up without any kind of warning and then start interrogating me about my personal life, yet I've heard nothing from you for months. Forgive me if I'm confused. Is this just a random visit?'

Drakon shook his head. He had planned how he was going to present this. To somehow build it up and carefully cushion the impact. To make it sound as if it was just part of life and he was dealing with it. He hadn't been expecting to just come out and say it— or for the words to taste like bitter poison when he spoke them.

'No. This wasn't a chance visit. I intended to come here today. It's Niko,' he grated. 'He's dead.'

Lucy blinked in confusion for his words made no sense. Because Niko was Drakon's twin brother. The wilder version of Drakon. Niko was the unpredictable twin—always had been. The volatile twin. The one who made headlines for all the wrong reasons and had almost been expelled from school an unbelievable three times. But although Niko was reckless he was also full of life. Why, she remembered him as the kind of man who was positively *bursting* with life.

'What are you talking about?' she said and afterwards wondered how she could have asked such a naïve question, in view of her own experience. 'How can he possibly be dead?'

Drakon's face contorted with darkness and pain and that was when she knew he was speaking the truth.

'He died of a drug overdose,' he bit out. 'Last month.'

Lucy gasped, her fingertips flying to her lips, her heart crashing wildly against her ribcage as she wondered how she could have been so stupid. Didn't she of all people know that young lives could be cut down like a blade of grass being sliced by a tractor at harvest time? Had she thought Drakon Konstantinou was immune to pain and loss, just because he was one of the world's richest men and was always flying around the globe on his private jet, brokering deals to add even more dollars to his already massive fortune?

She wanted to rush over to him. To fling her arms around his tense body and comfort him, as she had comforted innumerable grieving relatives on hospital wards in the past. But that was the trouble with sex. It changed things. You could never touch a former lover and pretend it was impartial, even if it was. 'Oh, Drakon,' she said, in a low voice, and could see from his blanched features and haunted eyes that he was in deep shock. 'I'm so sorry. I had no idea. Please. Won't you sit down? Let me get you something.' She looked around rather distractedly, trying to remember what was in the ancient drinks cabinet. 'I think I have some whisky somewhere—'

'I don't want whisky,' he said harshly.

She nodded. 'Okay. Then I'll make you some tea. Strong tea with lots of sugar. That's what you need.'

To her surprise he didn't object, just sank into one of the fireside armchairs, which looked too flimsy to be able to deal with his powerful frame, and Lucy sped into the kitchen, glad to have something to occupy herself with. Something to distract herself from her racing thoughts. But her hands were shaking so much that the china was chinking madly as she pulled cups and saucers down from one of the cupboards.

Sucking in a deep breath, she waited for the kettle to boil, wondering why she hadn't realised right from the beginning that something was wrong. Hadn't she been taught to read the telltale signs of body language which might have suggested that here was a man mourning the loss of his only sibling? While instead she had been selfishly preoccupied with her own battered ego, reflecting on the fact that he'd dumped her after a long week-end of wild and totally unexpected sex. What did something like that matter in the light of what he'd just told her?

She made the tea and frowned as she picked up the tray, because a nagging question still remained.

Why *had* he told her?

Slowly she went back into the tiny sitting room, her head still full of confusion. He turned to look at her and suddenly Lucy was scared by the expression on his rugged features. By the stony look which made his black eyes look so hard and bleak and cold—eyes which said quite clearly *you can't get close to me*. Scared too by another instinctive urge to run over and hug him, wondering if she was using his heartache as an excuse to touch him again. Because hadn't she yearned to stroke his silken flesh ever since he'd set her body on fire and made her realise what physical pleasure really meant?

She poured tea, dropping four sugar cubes into his cup and giving it a quick stir, before placing it on a small table beside the fire. Then she sat down in a chair opposite him, her knees pressed tightly together. 'Do you want to tell me about it?' she questioned softly. 'About what happened to Niko?'

Talking about it was the last thing Drakon wanted, but if he was to get Lucy to agree to his demands it was unavoidable. And how hard could it be to do that? He was a master of negotiation in the business world—surely he was able to employ the same tools of demand, cooperation and compromise in his personal life if he were to achieve what it was he wanted.

'How much do you know about my brother?' he questioned.

She hesitated, shrugging her shoulders

a little awkwardly. 'Not a lot. Once he left school he seemed to disappear off the radar.'

'*Neh*. That's a good way to describe what happened. He disappeared off the radar.' Drakon's voice grew distant and sounded as if it were coming from a long way off. But it was, he realised, with a jolt. It was coming from the past—and didn't they say that the past was like a different country? The Konstantinou twins, two black-eyed little boys, pampered like princes by a battery of servants yet overlooked by the wealthy parents who had employed those servants. They shared almost identical DNA and, for many years, few people could tell them apart, until they heard them speak. So similar in looks and yet so different in character. Sometimes they'd even been able to trick their own parents—but then, they'd lived such separate lives from their mother and father maybe that wasn't so surprising.

'Niko was the older of us—by just one and a half minutes—but those vital ninety seconds were all that were needed for him to be in line to inherit the family business. He thought he was going to be a very wealthy man—until the will was read and he discovered there was nothing left. All the money had gone.'

'How come?'

Drakon stared at her. Her bluebell eyes were a compassionate blur and for a moment he almost confided in her, until he drew himself short, reminding himself that certain segments of the past were irrelevant. He'd come here to talk about the future. 'The reasons don't matter,' he said, the words acrid on his lips. 'What is relevant is the way Niko coped with finding out the news, and the way he coped with it was with drugs. First it was a puff or two of dope at a party and then he started snorting cocaine, like so many of his buddies. But sooner or later, every addiction needs an additional boost because it isn't working any more.' His face twisted. 'And that's when he started on heroin.'

She didn't say anything. Had he expected her to? Had he secretly wanted her to come out with something trite and predictable so he could lash out as he had been wanting to lash out at someone for days now? He felt his jaw tighten as he continued with his story and yet somehow it was an unspeakable relief to unburden himself, because he hadn't really talked about this with anyone. Not even Amy.

He hadn't dared. Had he been afraid that describing his twin's fatal weakness might somehow reflect poorly on *him*? Might hold up a mirror to the cold darkness in his own soul and the guilt which gnawed away at him because he hadn't been there for his brother when he'd most needed him?

'I didn't find this out until afterwards,' he ground out. 'Because he left Greece and kept his distance from me—from everyone, really—and resisted every attempt I made to meet up. I only realised afterwards that he wanted to hide the true extent of his drug habit from me. If I'd known I might have been able to do something, but I didn't know. I guess I was too busy trying to make my fortune. Trying to recover something of the Konstantinou name and reputation.' He sighed. 'But eventually, I heard that Niko was living in Goa and was in a steady relationship and I can remember thinking that maybe things might be different. Personally, I've never believed in the transformative power of love— but that didn't mean I wasn't hopeful it might work for Niko.' His mouth twisted cynically and there was a pause. 'Apparently they had a beachside wedding and then I heard that she'd had a baby.'

'B-baby?' she echoed.

Drakon saw the colour drain from her face but still he didn't say it. It was as if he needed to mould the facts into some sort of recognisable structure before he hit her with the big one. Was he hoping to build up an element of sympathy, so she would find it impossible to say no to him? 'He got in touch with me just after the birth, to tell me I was now an uncle. He...he asked me if I wanted to go and meet Xander for myself and I told him I would. So I scheduled in a trip to go and see them the following week and was hopeful that the birth of a healthy child might bring him the kind of fulfilment he'd been unable to find elsewhere. Maybe it would have done if he and his wife hadn't decided to celebrate in their own time-honoured way. Not with a bottle of champagne or a candlelit dinner, but a lethal cocktail of narcotics.'

Her face blanched even more. 'Oh, no.'

'Oh, *neh*,' he agreed grimly. 'My partner was on a business trip nearby and some instinct made me ask her to check on them unannounced.' He paused, suddenly finding the words very difficult to say. 'Their bodies were still warm by the time she got there. I got a local investigator to find out what he could, and a little searching revealed that Niko's wife was as hooked on illegal substances as he was.'

'Oh, Drakon. I'm so sorry.'

He shook his head. 'We spoke to the doula who'd been attending her throughout the pregnancy and the only thing I'm grateful for is that she must have retained some vestige of common sense, and was able to give up drugs for the whole nine months.'

She flinched, the words spilling urgently from her mouth. 'And the baby?' she demanded. 'What about the baby?'

'Is unharmed,' he supplied grimly. 'The life force is powerful. He is lusty and strong and with his Greek nanny now—safe and warm not far from here, in London.' He felt his mouth twist, as if recounting words he didn't particularly want to say. 'You see, Niko and his wife had named me as the child's official guardian and so he is living with me.'

She leaned forward, clasping her hands together as if in prayer, an expression of earnestness on her face. But he could see indecision there, too, and she seemed to be choosing her words carefully. 'This is a heartbreaking story, Drakon—and I'm so sorry for your loss,' she breathed. 'But I'm still not quite sure why you're telling me all this.'

He stared at her. Was she really so naïve? Maybe she was. She'd certainly been *innocent* when he'd parted her thighs that hot summer evening and slid inside the unexpected tightness of her body. Though maybe he'd been the naïve one not to have realised that the wholesome Lucy Phillips had been untouched by another man. When he'd bumped into her in England she'd appeared almost invisible and the thought of seducing her couldn't have been further from his mind. And yet things had inexplicably turned sexual when he'd dropped in on her when she'd been staying on his island.

He remembered seeing her swimming in his pool, her strong arms arcing through the turquoise water in a graceful display of strength and power. Length after length he had watched her swim and when she'd eventually surfaced and blinked droplets of water from her eyes, she had looked genuinely surprised—and pleased—to see him. He shouldn't have been turned on by her plain and practical swimsuit but he had been, though maybe because he'd never seen someone of her age wearing something so old-fashioned. Just as he shouldn't have been unexpectedly charmed by the way she made him laugh—which was rare enough to be noteworthy. He'd found himself staying on for dinner, even though he hadn't planned to—and even though he'd told himself that her dress was cheap, that hadn't stopped him from being unable to tear his eyes away from the way the dark material had clung to her fleshy curves, had it?

Maybe it was inevitable that they had started kissing—and just as inevitable that they'd ended up having sex. The unexpected and unwanted factor had been encountering her intact hymen and realising he was the first man she'd ever been intimate with. At the time he'd been irritated by the fact she hadn't told him because, according to friends who knew about such things, taking a woman's virginity brought with it all kinds of problems—not least the kind of mindless devotion which was the last thing he needed. In fact, he despised it, for reasons which still made him shudder. His mouth hardened. He had enough difficulty keeping women at arm's length as it was, without some idealistic innocent longing for rose petals and wedding bells.

But his irritation had lasted no longer than

it took to resume his powerful rhythm inside her. And she had surprised him. Not just because she had proved to be an energetic and enthusiastic lover who had kissed more sweetly than any other woman he'd ever known. No. Because she seemed to have realised herself the limitations of their brief affair and to have accepted the fact that he had ghosted her from his life afterwards. She hadn't made any awkward phone calls or sent texts carefully constructed in order to appear 'casual'. And if his abundantly healthy ego had been fleetingly dented by her apparent eagerness to put what had happened behind her, the feeling had soon left him, because it was entirely mutual. But it made him realise that in many ways Lucy Phillips was exceptional. Emotionally independent, a trained midwife and, thus, the perfect candidate for what he needed…

He felt his mouth dry as he studied her earnest face and the clothes which failed to flatter her curvy shape. It was hard now to believe that she had choked out her fulfilment as he had driven into her firm body or to imagine the way he had fingered her nipples in the blazing Greek sunshine so that they had puckered into tight little nubs just ripe for sucking. But when you stopped to think about it, *all* of this was hard to believe and he needed to present his case so that she would receive it sympathetically. Rising to his feet, he addressed her stumbled question as he slowly approached her fireside chair. 'I'm telling you because I need your help, Lucy.'

'*My* help?' she echoed, her bright eyes looking up at him in surprise as his shadow enveloped her in darkness. 'Are you kidding? How on earth can I help someone like you when you're one of the richest men in the world and I have practically nothing?'

'No, I'm not kidding,' he negated firmly. 'And, far from having nothing, you have something I need very badly. Niko's baby needs security and continuity. He needs a home and I'm in a position to offer him one. But not on my own. Not as a single man whose work takes him to opposite sides of the world and who has no experience of babies, or children. And that's why I'm asking you to marry me, Lucy. To be my wife and the mother of my orphaned nephew.'

CHAPTER TWO

LUCY'S MOUTH FELL open as she stared into the face of the powerful Greek billionaire, the flickering firelight illuminating the ebony and gold of his rugged features. She couldn't believe what Drakon had just asked her and his question made her feel as if she was taking part in a dream. An extra-surreal dream. But surely he wouldn't be looking so serious if he hadn't meant it. 'You want *me* to marry you?' she verified slowly.

He nodded—though his brief frown suggested he didn't quite agree with her choice of words. 'I do.'

Lucy shook her hair and her heavy ponytail slithered like a thick rope against her back. Wasn't it crazy—and sad—how, in life, timing was everything? If her brother hadn't been in the wrong place at the wrong time, he would still be here. And if Drakon Konstantinou had asked her this very question a few months earlier, her reaction to it would have been totally different. Because when she'd returned home after her brief excursion to his island home—high on a mixture of raging hormones and a heady introduction to multiple orgasms—she had prayed for a scenario just like this. She'd nursed the unrealistic fantasy that what she and Drakon had shared had been special. Super-special. She had longed for him to suddenly decide his life was empty without her and that he wanted them to make a go of things. Why wouldn't she, when he was like every woman's dream man—despite his undeniable arrogance and detachment? When she'd always had a secret crush on him…

Of course that had never happened. He had cut her out of his life as abruptly as he had blazed into it again—at a school reunion where she'd been employed by Caro's Canapés, the local catering firm for which she worked. In her plain green dress, she'd been serving sandwiches just before the pin-drop silence which had followed Drakon Konstantinou's entrance into Milton school's famous and historic hall. She remembered the way all the other men had consciously or unconsciously pulled back their shoulders and sucked in their stomachs, as if to big themselves up or look taller. But it had been to no avail because the Greek tycoon had still dominated the vast room without even trying. Like a black star, dark brilliance had radiated from his powerful body and drawn every single eye to him. Yet for some crazy and inexplicable reason, he had been looking at *her*.

Lucy remembered blushing deeply as she'd offered him an egg and cress sandwich because she'd been acutely aware of the time, years ago, when he'd gashed his leg while rowing for the first team and, eager to be a nurse herself, she had been helping her mother, the school matron, in the school sanatorium. Drakon had been lying on a narrow trolley, with blood seeping from his gaping wound, and Lucy had thought how much it must hurt as her mother had dabbed at it with antiseptic. But he hadn't shown it. He hadn't even winced, not once. She'd given him her fingers to grip and he had opened his eyes and stared at her. Stared at her with eyes as black as the night. A ripple of something unfamiliar and exciting had whispered its way down her spine and she had never forgotten that feeling. She had been only fourteen at the time, and Drakon a crucial three years older—it had been Lucy's first experience of physical attraction towards a member of the opposite sex and it had stayed with her, all those years. Why, it had fired straight back into life when she had extended the silver platter of sandwiches towards him and met the velvety blackness of his eyes.

Was it her corresponding blush which had amused him—which had deepened when he'd pointed out, in his drawling Greek accent, that it was a rare thing to see a woman blush these days? Or was it simply curiosity which had made him hang around as the reunion was coming to an end, and the headmaster was imploring him to join him and his wife for supper? But Drakon hadn't stayed. Amid a torrent of thundering rain, he had insisted on giving her a lift home in his fancy car and naturally Lucy had been tongue-tied by all that opulence.

It had been pretty scary to discover that her crush on him was as powerful as ever, and slightly unsettling that she couldn't seem to keep her gaze from straying to the muscular thrust of his thighs. She remembered the potent rush of warmth deep at her core, which had made her feel both excited and a little bit embarrassed, because she wasn't the type of person who usually thought about stuff like that. She never really came across eligible men and certainly nobody of Drakon's calibre ever entered her life. Even the ones who were more her type tended to glance over her shoulder whilst chatting at parties, as if searching the room for someone more interesting to talk to.

Yet after the reunion, when the throaty car had slid to a halt outside her tiny riverside cottage, Drakon had turned to her and said, 'So how are you, Lucy? I mean, *really*?'

Was it the sense of what had sounded like genuine interest—something she suspected was rare for a man like him—which had made her blurt out everything which had been on her mind? Well, not *everything*. She'd missed out the part which explained why she'd given up her beloved job in midwifery—because the reasons for that made her feel even less of a woman, and who in their right mind would wish to do that in the presence of such a gorgeous man? Instead Lucy had found herself telling him about her brother in the army, who had lost his life in that awful conflict, just as her father had done in a different war before that. And how afterwards her mother had seemed to lose the will to live and had just faded away—like one of those dusky pink roses which bloomed in the lavish walled gardens of Milton school.

She remembered the deep frown which had crossed the tycoon's face as he'd studied her admittedly pale skin and told her that what she needed was a holiday in the sun. Had she explained that such luxuries were far beyond her grasp on her wages as a waitress, or had he just guessed? She wasn't sure. All she knew was that he had extended a careless invitation for her to holiday on his own personal Greek island.

'You actually own an island?' she remembered querying in disbelief.

'Sure.' He had glittered her a smile. 'And my house is empty a lot of the time. It's yours any time you want to use it.'

So she had gone. It had been an uncharacteristic response to what had probably just been a throwaway gesture on his part, but it had been too good an opportunity to miss. Although he had casually mentioned that his private jet was available, Lucy had scraped together enough money to fund a cheap flight to Athens instead and then caught the staff ferry to his private island of Prasinisos, with a pile of engrossing books to read. It had been the most impetuous thing she'd ever done and she wasn't sure what she had expected. She certainly hadn't expected Drakon to suddenly arrive on a glittering super-yacht the size of Jupiter later that day, when she was emerging from the swimming pool looking like a drowned rat. Nor for him to join her beside the aqua glitter of the infinity pool once she'd showered all the chlorine out of her hair and the fierce beat of the sun had made her feel all lazy and laid-back.

For a while she'd said nothing, because instinct had told her he was a man who valued silence, and gradually she had seen Drakon relax—something she'd suspected he didn't do very often. He'd shown her the faint scar from the gash on his leg which she'd helped her mother to suture all those years ago, and something about that distant memory had made them both laugh. She remembered their eyes meeting and something intangible shimmering in the air around them. Lucy had been inexperienced, innocent and slightly out of her depth—all those things, yes. But she had also been excited and eager for what had happened later, after a delicious dinner on the terrace once his housekeeper had gone home.

For Drakon to fold her into his arms and kiss her and then kiss her some more. It had been as if her every dream had come true in that moment. As if her body had been poised on the brink of something very beautiful.

She'd thought he would quickly get bored with someone who wasn't at all experienced but her tongue's tentative exploration of his mouth had caused a low growl of pleasure to rumble up from his throat. He'd held her so tight that her soft body had moulded into the muscular hardness of his, so that when he had carried her off to his bedroom it had felt nothing but right. Even that slight awkwardness when he had stilled inside her and momentarily glared at her hadn't lasted longer than a couple of seconds.

The following morning she had woken naked in his bed and he had brought her dark coffee, which was thick and sweet, before taking her in his arms again, and the next few days had passed by in a sensual blur. He'd made love to her on the terrace, and in the cabin of his yacht as he'd sailed her round his island and showed her all the little bays and coves. He'd fed her grapes and trickled Greek honey onto a belly which had quivered as he'd licked it off.

And three days later it had all been over, without anything actually being said. There had been no awkward conversation or protracted farewells. He hadn't insulted her by telling her that his diary was too jam-packed for him to be able to see her again. He'd just given her a deep kiss, said goodbye and dropped her off at the airport by helicopter so at least she hadn't had to endure that rather bumpy ferry ride back to Athens. She hadn't heard a squeak from him since and, once she'd realised it wasn't going to happen, her hurt and disappointment had gradually faded into the recesses of her mind, because Lucy was nothing if not practical. She'd told herself to remember all the good bits and she'd tried not to have unrealistic expectations, because that way you could avoid hurt and disappointment as much as possible. She had been getting on with her life—her rather ordinary and predictable life—until the Greek tycoon had blazed back into it with the most implausible suggestion she'd ever heard!

'I can't believe you're asking me to marry you,' she breathed.

'Well, believe it,' he returned softly. 'Because it's true.'

'But why me?' she questioned, wishing that

her heart would stop thundering. 'There must be a million women who would make a more suitable wife for a man like you.'

He didn't even pay her the compliment of pretending to consider her remark and certainly didn't bother to deny it, just answered with a bluntness which somehow managed to be supremely insulting.

'There are indeed,' he agreed. 'In fact, if I were to measure suitability in terms of sophistication and familiarity with my world, you would be right at the back of the queue, Lucy.'

She swallowed. 'You don't pull your punches, do you, Drakon?'

'Do you think I should?' he mused. 'I've always been of the mindset that life is too short for prevarication and Niko's death has only confirmed that.'

He paused and as his night-dark gaze shimmered over her, Lucy wanted to tell him not to look at her like that—yet the craziest thing of all was that she wanted him to carry on doing it and never stop.

'I've never wanted to marry anyone nor have children of my own,' he said. 'Despite the fact that I have a vast fortune just waiting for someone to inherit.'

'Why not?' she asked quietly.

His black gaze seared into her, as if he was deciding how much to tell her. 'Because I don't believe in love. It's something I've never felt nor wanted to feel. To my mind, love is nothing but an invention which seems designed to excuse the most outrageous forms of behaviour.' His black eyes narrowed. 'But now I have an heir whether I like it or not and, because I am a twin, this child almost completely carries half my genes. So in a way, I have a ready-made family. I may not have wanted or planned it but now that I have it, I will make the best of it because that is how I operate. Providing Xander with a suitable mother and giving him some sort of grounding is the least I can do to try to compensate for such a horrible start to his young life. And while you may not have much money or be familiar with the world's high spots, you have something which makes you extra-special, Lucy.'

'Really? And what might that be?' Lucy's heart quickened, though afterwards she would be ashamed of her needy desire to have him shower praise on her, because it didn't happen. Instead, he listed her credentials like an employer telling her why she had surprisingly beaten the other candidates.

'You're a trained nurse for a start,' he drawled, his Greek accent deep and velvety. 'A midwife as I recall, which makes you extra-suitable. And you are both pure and respectable, if what I discovered about you back in the summer was anything to go by. Once I started considering you for the role, I realised that your virginity was actually a great asset.'

He didn't seem to notice that his last remark had made her cheeks grow heated. Of course he didn't. He was talking *at* her instead of *to* her, wasn't he? He didn't really care about her thoughts and reactions—nor about the fact that he was making her sound like an upmarket brand of soap. To Drakon Konstantinou she was nothing more than a commodity.

'Rather than being a bit of a bore, which was how you seemed to regard it at the time?' she questioned rather snappily.

'Yes, you could put it like that,' he said, without missing a beat. 'Your purity now takes on an entirely different aspect, Lucy, and it has become important to me. It's an indication of the way you've lived your life. You haven't had a vast number of lovers before me, and such reserve is rare among women.'

'But what difference does my lifestyle make to what you have in mind?' she questioned. 'Why does it matter that I was a virgin?'

His mouth had hardened so that suddenly it resembled a savage slash across the lower part of his face and she could see coldness and calculation enter his black eyes.

'Because you will be able to lead by example. I want an old-fashioned woman with old-fashioned values and you are the perfect fit. This baby carries the genes of two addicts who were willing to put their own pleasure before his welfare,' he continued bitterly. 'Not only do I need to ensure that never happens again, I also need to stack the odds in Xander's favour from now on.'

Lucy didn't say anything. Not straight away. Not when he was looking so forbidding and so...*angry*—though she realised he was angry with his brother and not with her. She rose to her feet from the fireside chair because she felt at a psychological disadvantage having to stare up at him like that and it was making her neck ache. And she needed to put some distance between them. Some very necessary distance to get her thoughts in order. Away from the spell of his proximity and coercive weave of his words.

She walked over to the opposite side of the small room and stared out of the window at the river. The moon was beginning to rise and was forming a dappled silvery path on the darkening water and she could see that a cottage on the opposite bank must have put up their Christmas tree. She blinked as she stared at the glittering lights—rose and gold and green and blue—but felt none of the prescribed magic as she turned to meet Drakon's hooded gaze. 'Isn't the normal thing in these kind of circumstances to employ a nanny?' she questioned. 'Which you already have done, by the sound of it. You can afford to engage a whole battery of staff, Drakon. Why do you need a wife?'

He shook his head, like a man who had all the answers—but hadn't he always seemed like a man with all the answers? 'Obviously the child will need a full-time nanny and Sofia is eager to continue in that role,' he said, and paused. 'But that isn't the point, Lucy.'

'Isn't it?' she asked quietly.

'No.'

He shook his head and Lucy could see the

bleakness in his eyes. She thought how *empty* his face looked. As if he'd been drained of all emotion so that he resembled some dark and forbidding statue. As if his body were composed of cold marble instead of flesh and blood, and a sudden trepidation whispered over her skin as she realised there was no real warmth in this man. 'I don't understand,' she breathed.

'Then let me make it clearer for you. I don't want this child to grow up in that kind of world—the adopted child of a single billionaire,' he bit out. 'I don't want him looked after by a series of employees with no emotional investment in his future, like I was. I don't want him sent away to school like I was. Xander needs a family. A real family.'

Lucy swallowed, wondering which of them was being naïve now. Did anyone truly know what a *real* family was—or did they all just rely on the slushy default version you saw in films, or read about in books, with people clustered round a fire, throwing their heads back in mutual laughter? Yet having a family was the bedrock of society, wasn't it? It was the dream which the majority of people aspired to, even if the reality was often so different. Was he really suggesting that the legal union of two people who had briefly been lovers could magically create some sort of fairy-tale household?

But then her mind began to focus on something else. On a single word the Greek tycoon had just uttered and which now lodged itself deep in her mind.

Xander.

Xander, his nephew and innocent little baby.

A motherless baby.

Lucy's heart clenched with a pain she should have anticipated because unwittingly Drakon had stumbled across her Achilles heel. The reason why she always felt as if something inside her was missing and incomplete. The one part of her life which could never be fulfilled, unless...

Her mouth dried.

Unless she was brave enough—or crazy enough—to accept the billionaire's bizarre offer. Because wasn't he offering her the magic-wand solution she had once yearned for in the form of instant motherhood? Her mind began to race. Could it work? Could she provide what little Xander needed—and in so doing gain for herself what she thought had been lost for ever?

Take it slowly, she told herself firmly. *Slowly.*

'This sounds like a very long-term plan,' she suggested carefully.

'It is.' Some of the coldness had left his face and in its place she could see conviction. And persuasion. 'I'm talking endurance, Lucy. About putting a child's needs first and making a promise to each other that neither of us intends to break. About commitment and stability.'

'How can you be so sure you could find that with me?' She stared at him. 'When you don't really *know* me. At school you were years ahead of me. I was just the school nurse's daughter who was allowed to take certain classes with the boys. Apart from those times when you were having the wound on your leg attended to, you didn't even notice me. We were just ships which passed in the night and, apart from that, we've only spent a few days together.'

'You think that time we spent on Prasinisos didn't provide me with the opportunity to discover something of what makes Lucy Phillips tick?' he enquired softly.

Lucy wanted to turn away from the mocking look in his eyes but that would be an immature response to a perfectly reasonable question. Because they *had* been intimate—and it would be hypocritical to pretend they hadn't.

'I can't deny we were lovers,' she husked. 'But physical intimacy during a mini-break on a Greek island is one thing. Real life is another. We're strangers, Drakon. How do you know I wouldn't drive you crackers before the first month was up?'

His eyes narrowed but Lucy couldn't mistake the brief flash of surprise which had gleamed there. As if he couldn't quite believe that she was prevaricating instead of instantly accepting his offer.

And wasn't there a part of her which couldn't quite believe it herself? Making out as if there were men lining up and asking her to marry them every day of the week!

'We would have to work at it, in the way that people with arranged marriages have always done,' he said. 'And we will be walking into it with our eyes open—without any of the myths of love and romance which set people up for disappointment, and failure. If we refuse to have unrealistic expectations about each other, then we should succeed.' He slanted her a smile. 'Does that reassure you?'

Lucy thought how clever he was. And how controlling, too. That slow smile—she was certain—had been angled at her deliberately in order to pump up her heart rate and it had worked, hadn't it? Was that the main reason he was here—because he thought of her as passive? Wasn't it time to demonstrate that while she might be poor and unglamorous, that didn't necessarily mean she was a complete pushover? 'So what's in it for me, Drakon?' she questioned. 'What made you think you could turn up without warning and ask me to become your wife? Were you so certain I'd say yes?'

Drakon's eyes narrowed. He felt a certain responsibility towards her because he had unwittingly taken her virginity and had quashed his desire to see her again because he'd known he was capable of hurting her. He'd suspected that someone like her would be unable to cope with a commitment-phobe like him, even though he'd been sorely tempted to have sex with her again. But that had been back then—when his life had been free and unfettered. This was now, when he had an unexpected burden of responsibility to shoulder.

His mouth hardened. 'I had an idea you might be tempted.'

'Because?'

Would it be cruel to point out that without him a limited future inevitably beckoned for someone like her? But wouldn't any future be limited compared with the one he was offering her with all the money she could ever desire? He looked once again at her bare fingers. 'You don't show any signs of settling down,' he observed.

'Not at the moment, no.'

'So do you see yourself continuing to make ends meet as a relatively hard-up waitress?' he mused. 'Is that how you want the rest of your life to pan out?'

There was anger on her face now. And something which looked like pride. 'I don't just waitress. I actually help Caroline with all the cooking,' she declared icily. 'And she's indicated that she'd be prepared to let me buy the business when she eventually retires, which is what I've been saving up for. The waitressing is just a means to an end.'

'And that's what you really want, is it, Lucy? Resigning yourself to a life of relative poverty. Of a futile wait for Mr Right, perhaps—'

'Excuse me?' She pulled back her shoulders and glared at him. 'You think all women are just waiting around for a would-be husband to leap into their life?'

He gave a careless shrug. 'I'm saying that plenty of them are, yes—at least, in my experience. But if that's what you're hoping for, let me enlighten you. That man is just fantasy. He's someone who may or may not materialise,' he said softly. 'Whereas a rich man with whom you're sexually compatible—a man who really needs you—he's here. Right here.'

His words had got through to her, he could see that. Just as he could see the temptation which flickered in her blue eyes.

'And if I were to agree...' Her voice tailed off. 'What kind of marriage would you expect?'

Drakon heard the uncertain note in her voice but her darkening eyes told a different story. And suddenly he found himself being sucked into a vortex of erotic recall. He remembered the softness of her thighs and the untamed bush of hair which concealed her untouched treasure. For perhaps the only time in his adult sexual life, he had been momentarily astonished—and not just because she hadn't waxed—because what woman of twenty-eight was a virgin in this day and age? He remembered the soft gasp she'd given when he had entered her, the faint pain of her initial response quickly giving way to breathless murmurs of encouragement and then, to her first sweetly sobbing orgasm. And hadn't that felt sublime? Hadn't he experienced a deep satisfaction as she had choked out her pleasure against his bare shoulder, her ecstatic response filling him with a rush of primeval pleasure?

He'd made love to her countless times during those few short days—justifying his seemingly insatiable appetite with the assurance that he was simply enjoying introducing her to sex. But it had been more than that, even though he'd been loath to admit it then and was even less inclined to do so now. Her untutored eagerness had lit a strange yearning inside him—one which was being ignited right now.

He felt the exquisite throb of desire at his groin and heard the powerful thunder of his own heart. Maybe it was wrong to be thinking about sex at a time like this, but didn't they say the life force was at its most powerful during periods of grief and loss? Wasn't it nature's way of sustaining the human race, as well as reinforcing that, while his twin brother might be lying cold and dead beneath the hard earth, he, Drakon, was very much alive and at the mercy of his senses?

He began to walk towards her, noticing the instinctive tremble of her lips as he grew closer, but she didn't stop him, nor show any signs of wanting to. She just stood there, her blue eyes bright and questioning, her thick dark hair spilling out of the untidy plait which snaked down her back.

'I would expect the usual things which marriage entails,' he said huskily. 'Physical intimacy, for a start. I think that's one thing we both know we really do have in common.'

Distractedly, Lucy rubbed her toe against the rug, scarcely able to believe they were having this kind of conversation. Normally she didn't have to deal with anything more taxing than someone asking whether there were any gluten-free sandwiches available. Yet Drakon Konstantinou had just come right out and told her they were sexually compatible—him with a vast cast of ex-lovers and her with only one! She had no experience of such things but instinct told her that his words were true.

But was it *enough* for her to accept his offer of marriage? Enough for her to turn her back on her old life and enter a new one, which might be exciting but was tinged with uncertainty? With a father and a brother in the military she had grown up surrounded by uncertainty and she'd hated it. She'd longed for a safer world. A more predictable world. It was one of the reasons why she'd never really made waves in her own adult life. Why she'd always followed the rules and played safe.

Until she'd bumped into Drakon Konstantinou one balmy summer evening and the world had spun on its axis.

She knew she should say no. She should retreat back into her comfortable little world and try to forget the sexy billionaire and his bizarre offer.

But Lucy had been badly affected by what had happened to her family. In a few short years it had been wiped out as if it had never existed. Her father, brother and mother had all died in relatively quick succession. Orphaned and alone, she'd felt as if she had no real place anywhere. Sometimes she'd felt invisible. She still did. As if people were looking right through her. And all these feelings were compounded by the fact that she could never have children and be able to create a family of her own.

She stared into Drakon's rugged face, hope flaring inside her despite all her misgivings. Because the Greek tycoon was offering her exactly that. Something she'd once thought impossible but which, unlike him, she *had* wanted. An instant family. A baby to love and to care for. Her mouth dried. Could it work? Could she *make* it work? And by doing that give them both what they needed—he a wife and she a child?

She licked her lips. 'When do you need an answer by?'

'I don't see any point in waiting. I am a man who likes to settle a deal as quickly as possible. Now would be ideal.'

She shook her head. 'Now is too soon, Drakon. I need a few days to process this. To mull over everything you've said and decide whether or not it could work. It's too big a consideration to just toss you an answer.'

His black eyes narrowed and in them Lucy could see speculation.

'Of course, there's another factor which needs to be considered. I'd hate you to overlook that, Lucy.'

She asked the question without really thinking about it. 'Which is what?'

He gave a slow smile. 'Use your imagination.'

The dip in his voice and the suddenly smoky light in his eyes made Lucy realise he was going to touch her and on one level she recognised that it was studied and manipulative. But it still worked, because Drakon knew how to press all her buttons. Even though an inner voice was urging caution, Lucy let him pull her in his arms to kiss her and, oh, she was hungry for that kiss.

So hungry.

Her fingers coiled around his broad shoulders as the voice of reason tried to warn her this was only going to confuse matters. But her body was refusing to listen to reason— its hungry demands silencing every sensible objection. Because this was amazing. Sweet sensations were flooding her body and her newly awoken sexual appetite—honed by five months of aching absence—made her think she might faint if Drakon didn't quell this sudden urgent need inside her.

His hand drifted up underneath her baggy sweater, his fingers encountering the shivering flesh of her torso before moving upwards to cup the straining mound of her breast. It was exquisite torture to feel her nipple pushing greedily against the lace of her bra, and all the while his lips were gently prising hers open. Exploring. Probing. Making her melt with the sensual flicker of his tongue. Making her writhe her hips in wordless appeal. She could feel the tension in his powerful body as he levered one powerful thigh between hers and it eased some of the pressure, even as it managed to build some more. She could feel the hardness at his groin. A hard ridge pressing urgently against the immaculate cut of his trousers, which told her graphically just how much he wanted her. She should have felt shy but that was the last thing she was feeling and Lucy knew that if the Greek had ripped off her jeans and panties before positioning himself where she was aching most, she would have taken him deep inside her.

'Drakon,' she choked out.

But her words seemed to shatter the spell as, abruptly, the kissing stopped. Moving his head away, he rocked back on his heels, inscrutable black eyes searching her face intently, and Lucy could see a nerve flickering at his temple. Had he decided he didn't want her after all? she wondered wildly. Had that rapid near-seduction been a demonstration of his power over her, rather than real desire? And did that mean he was about to withdraw his offer of marriage?

'Yes, I want you very much,' he said, scarily answering her unspoken question before directing a rueful glance at his watch. 'But now is not the time. Nor the place. Not when my car is waiting and I have a raft of meetings I need to attend. But it will keep.'

'K-keep?' she echoed.

'Neh,' he agreed, glittering her a sudden smile. 'I've never been married before, Lucy. I've never wanted to be part of such a flawed institution, if the truth were known. But if I am to be your husband—which I fully intend to be—then there will be plenty of opportunity for lovemaking. And don't they say that hunger is the best aphrodisiac of all?'

All the time he was speaking, his fingertip was tracing a line along the edges of her lips and Lucy hated the way her mouth quivered in response. Just as she hated his arrogant assumption that she would be his wife when she hadn't given him her decision. 'But I haven't said I'll marry you yet. And I can't do that until I've met baby Xander,' she added firmly.

A look of calculation entered his black eyes. 'The key word is *"yet",'* he observed silkily. 'For it indicates that your acceptance is simply a matter of time. We both know that.' His black eyes glittered. 'Because you will marry me, Lucy. Not just because I can reward you with the things most people spend their lives craving, but because you are in a position to help a vulnerable little baby as no other person could do right now. But that's not all. You will marry me because you want me and the only way you're going to have me is by agreeing to become my wife.'

CHAPTER THREE

THERE WAS BARELY any room for the limousine to make its way down the icy lane and Lucy's heart was hammering as she locked the door of her cottage and made her way towards the luxury car. She looked around at the leafless trees and frosty bushes as if committing them to memory one last time—because who knew when she would be back?

Inadvertently she cracked through an icy puddle and mud sloshed onto her newly polished boots as Drakon's chauffeur opened the door of the car, her tentative smile being met with nothing more than a deferential nod. As she slid onto the back seat she could feel her anxiety grow and the doubts which had been bugging her for days threatened to overwhelm her. She thought about the way Drakon had kissed her and the way her body had responded so hungrily. She thought about his track record with women and her own miserable tally of just one lover. She thought about how detached and indifferent he could seem, except when engaged in some form of sensual contact and a very real fear washed over her as she realised she was entering territory which was completely alien to her.

You don't have to do this, she told herself. *It's not too late to pull out. Nobody's forcing you to become the Greek tycoon's wife. If he can't get you to look after his orphaned nephew then his money will buy him the best care in the world. It isn't your responsibility.*

For a split second she thought about jumping out of the car. About rushing back to the sanctuary of her cottage and emailing Drakon to tell him she couldn't go through with it. But then the limousine's powerful engine fired into life and they were on their way to London and suddenly it was too late for Lucy to change her mind. And wasn't the truth of it that deep down she didn't want to, for all kinds of reasons? It certainly wasn't the lure of the Greek tycoon's glamorous lifestyle which was calling to her. She'd seen enough rich boys at the boarding school where her mother had worked to know that money certainly didn't come with a guarantee of happiness. The thought of having a baby and a family of her own was the most powerful motivator, of course it was—but there was something else, too. Something which was much more intangible, and that was the way Drakon made her feel whenever he touched her. As if she were real. As if she were capable of things she'd never imagined she could do. It was a heady feeling but it was tinged with a danger she didn't quite yet understand.

All through the journey to the capital, she tried to relax, trying her best to keep her boots from smearing mud on the pristine leather interior. Not for the first time she wondered what had happened to one of her suede moccasins, which had mysteriously gone missing—and it was something of a relief to be able to think about something unconnected to Drakon as she tried to work out exactly what had happened to it. Once she had exhausted all possibilities she tried to concentrate on the landscape which was rushing past the tinted windows, but her busy thoughts ensured that most of what she saw remained a blur until they reached the centre of London. And that was when Lucy blinked in surprise, feeling as if she'd emerged from her countryside bubble to arrive in a city she scarcely recognised.

Because Christmas was all around and it was as if the entire city had been taken over by Disney. The big stores were shiny with tinsel and glitter and fake snow. Red-clothed Santas with fluffy white beards rocked manically as little children pressed their noses against the plate-glass windows. Past the giant tree on Trafalgar Square the luxury car purred and when they stopped at some traffic lights, Lucy opened one of the windows slightly so she could hear the carol singers who were collecting money for the homeless. Her heart clenched as she registered the first notes of 'Silent Night' because it always reminded her of her brother, and quickly she pressed the button so that the electric window floated up to blot out the nostalgic carol. Instead she focussed on the crowds of people who all seemed to be on a mission, hell-bent on buying gifts even though there were several weeks left until the big day.

There were plenty of things Lucy liked about Christmas. The lights. The colours. The music. The way usually inhibited people went out of their way to smile and say hello. She just didn't like the way it made her *feel*, because it seemed to emphasise all the things she didn't have. It was a time when you could

feel extra-lonely if you lived on your own because most people seemed to have somebody,
while she had nobody. It was when she most
missed having a family. When she found herself feeling emotionally vulnerable—which
wasn't a particularly nice sensation. Usually
she tucked herself away with a large supply
of chocolate and sobbed her way through just
about every corny film which was showing
on TV.

But this year was going to be different. Her
teeth pressed down hard on her bottom lip
and she gnawed away at it. And how. She
had a wedding to organise and—this was the
bit she still couldn't get her head around—
she was going to be a Christmas bride. At
least, that was the plan—although nothing
had been arranged just yet, which was making the thought of marrying Drakon seem
even more surreal than it already was. Excite-
ment and dread flooded through her, yet the
truth was that, despite her misgivings about
becoming the Greek tycoon's wife, she had
stumbled at the first hurdle. She had fallen
in love with his orphaned nephew.

Her throat thickened as she remembered
meeting the tiny baby—a meeting on which
everything had hinged. She had insisted on

Drakon being absent. Had she been afraid he would influence her? That he would distract her with his powerful presence and remind her of how much she still wanted *him*? She had expected objections from the powerful tycoon. She'd imagined he might wish to observe her first contact with his tiny nephew as a kind of interactive job interview, but to her surprise he had agreed to stay away. She'd been jittery with nerves—because the thought of holding a baby again after so long had thrown up all kinds of complicated emotions. Alone, she had waited in one of the reception rooms of Drakon's vast London apartment until the nanny had appeared with a snowy white bundle in her arms. Greek-born Sofia must have been in her fifties, though her step was spritely as she carried the baby towards Lucy.

And Lucy remembered the compassion which had washed over her as she'd stared down at Xander's tiny head and it had been pure instinct which had made her extend her arms so that she could cradle the infant close to her racing heart. She had been prepared for the pain which had speared through her at the thought that she would never hold a child of her own like this, but not for the instant bonding which had followed. Had it been provoked by tenderness for one who had lost so much at such an early age, or by the tiny starfish hand which had clutched her extended finger and melted her heart?

She had asked if she could give the baby his bottle and then cuddled him until he had fallen asleep. And soon after Sofia had taken Xander back to the nursery, Lucy's telephone had rung, as if it had been programmed to do so.

'Well?'

Drakon's question had been terse and to the point and there had seemed little point in prevaricating. Why pretend that this was anything other than a cold-blooded business arrangement?

'Yes.' Lucy's voice had been low but unfaltering. 'I will be your wife.'

'Good.' There was a pause. 'In which case, you need to pack a case and I'll send a car to collect you. Be ready tomorrow morning.'

'So soon?'

'What's the point of waiting, Lucy? Delay will serve little purpose.'

'But I've got three cocktail parties next week for Caro's Canapés which I'm booked to work at.'

'Leave that to me. I will arrange a suitable replacement.' His voice had dipped to become a murmured caress. 'I intend for you to become my wife as quickly as possible and I think we both know the reason for that.'

Lucy had opened her mouth to say something and then shut it again. Because didn't she want that too? Wasn't there a tiny part of her which worried that if they left it too long, Drakon might suddenly change his mind and realise that it was a completely preposterous idea to marry someone like her? And wasn't it crazy to realise how gutted she would be if that were the case? 'No, tomorrow sounds absolutely fine,' she said compliantly.

Which was why she was now on her way to Drakon's Mayfair apartment and her brand-new life. Trying not to feel like Cinderella as she perched on the edge of the limousine's soft leather seat and attempted to keep her muddy boots elevated.

Her heart was pounding as they skirted Hyde Park and drove towards the imposing modern block in Mayfair, which commanded a prime view of the city's largest park. Lucy peered out of the window, her heart missing a beat as she saw Drakon's imposing figure imprinted darkly against the glittering windows of the block. She blinked in surprise. He was waiting, she realised. Waiting for *her*?

He seemed lost in thought and hadn't noticed the car, giving Lucy the opportunity to study him unobserved. She thought that seeing him standing on the street made him seem even more of a stranger than he already was. She noticed a blonde wearing dark glasses and a fur coat do a double-take as she walked past him with a tiny white dog trotting on a red lead, though unfortunately the dog chose that precise moment to cock its little leg against a lamppost. Yet wasn't that the type of sleek woman he *should* have selected as his wife? Lucy wondered painfully, trying and failing not to drink him in with her hungry gaze.

On the cold winter day, he was dressed entirely in black and the effect was to make him dominate his surroundings even more than usual. The inky overcoat echoed the dark gleam of his eyes but his mouth was hard and unsmiling. He'd had his hair cut and the rock-star strands were now neatly trimmed in a style which seemed to emphasise all his olive-skinned beauty. Suddenly she realised he could make her blood sing even from this distance away, although the day was so cold and wintry. Being around him was like having a *fever*, she thought, clasping her fingers together so tightly that the knuckles cracked.

Some sort of notification must have gone off, for he slid his phone from his inside pocket and glanced down at it, then narrowed his black eyes to focus on the approaching limousine. Had he been forewarned that she was on her way, perhaps by his taciturn driver? In desperation, Lucy glanced down to see that her hands were shaking and a sudden shiver of trepidation whispered over her skin before she dared lift her head to meet his gaze. Was she imagining the faint flash of disapproval in his eyes as the car purred to a halt and he moved forward to open the door for her?

A cold gust of wind whipped through her as she stepped onto the pavement, acutely aware of the fact that her best coat was looking decidedly threadbare and that, although she'd spent an hour last night buffing up her boots, their newfound shine didn't hide the fact that they were old. She'd tried to do her best with her appearance but her resources were limited and even if they hadn't been— what *did* a poor girl wear when she was about to move in with her billionaire fiancé? She felt like diving back into the car and begging the driver to take her home, but somehow she managed to scrabble together a memory—an important thing she'd learnt on her very first day on the wards as a student nurse. And afterwards, whenever her mother had sunk into one of her deep depressions and Lucy had attempted to help her spirits up. *Keep it positive. Look on the bright side.*

'So,' she said brightly, tilting her chin upwards and managing a faint reproduction of a smile. 'Here I am.'

Yes. Here she was. Drakon tensed as he felt a rush of something he didn't recognise. Was it incredulity that he'd selected this woman to be his bride when she couldn't have looked like a more unlikely candidate if she'd tried? But he'd had no choice. And wasn't that the story of his life? he reminded himself grimly. That unwanted responsibilities were always waiting in the shadows to grab at him and to direct his life onto a path he had never intended…

Her big blue eyes were looking at him uncertainly and something made him dip his head to brush his lips over hers in a fleeting kiss, amused by her instinctive intake of breath and the sudden confusion of her expression, as if she hadn't been expecting him to embrace her so publicly. In truth, he hadn't been expecting it himself, but he found himself turned on by the fact she wasn't wearing any make-up and by the provocative tremble of her lips. Maybe he should take her inside and kiss her a little more thoroughly, so that she would lose that rather unflattering look of apprehension and replace it with one of passion instead.

'Let's go inside,' he said abruptly. Drawing away, he ushered her into the luxury complex, past the security guard who was regarding her with open curiosity.

'What about my suitcase?' she was saying as they reached the elevator and the doors slid open.

'What about it?'

'I've left it in the car.'

'The driver will bring it inside shortly. You don't have to worry about things like that any more, Lucy.' Rather impatiently, he pressed the button. 'You'll find my staff will deal with the more humdrum elements of your life from now on and you won't have to bother with logistics. So why don't you just concentrate on getting to know one of your new homes?'

'One of them?' she affirmed breathlessly.

The wave of his hand was careless. Sometimes he forgot that the extent of his wealth was remarkable to most people and he supposed he should be grateful that his new fiancée hadn't already tallied up all his properties with greedy anticipation. 'I have homes in New York and Athens as well as this one,' he drawled. My Greek island villa you have already seen, of course.'

'Of course,' she said.

He watched as she fixed her eyes imploringly on the bright red arrow indicating their progress towards his penthouse apartment, as if she was finding the confined space in the elevator claustrophobic. *You and me both,* he thought unwillingly, his attention drawn to the curves of her body, which her thin grey coat couldn't quite disguise. He could feel the pump of his heart and the throb at his groin and wondered whether he should rid himself of some of the frustration which had been building up inside him for days now. But thoughts of seduction were vanquished by the words which burst from her lips almost as if she hadn't planned to say them, her blue eyes suddenly darkening so that they looked as blue as a Grecian sea.

'I wasn't…' She drew in a deep breath. 'To

be honest I wasn't expecting to see you until this evening. I thought you'd be working.'

Surely that wasn't disappointment he could hear in her soft English voice? A flicker of a smile touched the edges of Drakon's lips. Maybe there was more fire to Lucy Phillips than he had initially given her credit for. 'I had a rare window in my diary and I thought it might be less daunting if I was here to greet you myself,' he explained as the elevator reached the penthouse and the doors slid open.

'That's very kind of you.'

'Make the most of it. I'm not usually known for my kindness,' he informed her drily. 'Come on in.'

Obediently, she followed him into the reception room, and he thought how much she resembled a new member of staff as she stood nervously in the centre of his modern London apartment with its bird's-eye view over the park. But in a way, that was exactly what she was. As his wife, she would be fulfilling her prescribed role just as adequately as one of his chefs, or drivers, or housekeepers. And wasn't her trepidation one of the reasons he had chosen to marry her? She was both compliant and inexperienced and because of that he could mould her into the kind of spouse he wanted her to be, just as he would train up a new assistant.

'It's huge,' she commented.

'But you've been here before. When you met Xander.'

'Yes. That's right. But I only saw the nursery areas. I had no idea there was this other huge section.' She looked around, cocking her head to one side as if listening for something. 'Where *is* Xander?'

Drakon still wasn't used to having the baby around and he frowned, trying to remember. 'Sofia has taken him to the doctor for some sort of routine check. At least, I think that's what she said.'

She sucked in a deep breath. 'You didn't consider it might be better if I could have gone along as well? If I'm to be his, well, his…mother.'

Something unknown clutched at Drakon's heart like a vice. Was it anger that his brother should have treated his son with such a failure of care and cast him into the unwanted role of father? Or fear that he would be incapable of giving this child any true affection, as his own father had been unable to give him? With an effort, he pushed the bitter memories away—for what good would they serve him now?

'There will be plenty of time for you to play happy families, Lucy. First things first. Let me show you around properly and then I have a surprise for you.'

'I'm not crazy about surprises,' she warned him lightly.

'I think you'll like this one,' he promised.

Lucy thought how arrogant he sounded. Did that mean she was going to have to *pretend*? To smooth the way for their future marriage by showing him gratitude at all times? Would that be the grown-up way to proceed?

She began to follow him through the huge apartment, trying and failing to remember the precise configuration of the rooms. But she would quickly learn where everything was, she reassured herself—despite the fact that the entire ground floor of her riverside cottage would have fitted into one of the en suite bathrooms! One of the vast reception rooms led into a book-lined study, which looked more like a public library and contained leather-bound volumes in both English and Greek. There was an enormous kitchen with an adjoining dining room, three big en suite bedrooms on one side of the wide corridor, as well as the nursery suite on the other, which was completely self-contained.

'I've given you your own bedroom,' he said as his footsteps halted. 'I decided it would be more appropriate if we slept apart until the wedding. Something befitting the status of my relatively innocent fiancée.' His black eyes gleamed. 'That doesn't mean we cannot be intimate or imaginative, of course.'

'Oh?'

'I'll be right next door,' he informed her. 'It will be like a throwback to a different age. I cannot tell you how much the novelty of that appeals to me, Lucy.'

Lucy's breasts had grown heavy at his provocative words but her erotic recall was forgotten the moment he pushed open the bedroom door. Her lips fell open but she barely noticed the amazing view or huge bed, or the superb painting of a tiny fishing village which looked suspiciously like the one on his private island. All she could see were the piles of clothes which were *everywhere*, making the room look more like the changing room of an upmarket department store than a bedroom. There were sleek dresses hanging in front of the built-in cupboards and a gorgeous plum-coloured coat with a velvet collar. One of the cupboards was open and inside she could see colour-coordinated lines of beautiful silky shirts, and skirts which varied from pencil to flounce. Further along the rail were more casual clothes—cashmere sweaters which bore little resemblance to her own hand-knits and denim jeans which she was doubtful she'd be able to slide over her curvy hips. This must be the surprise he'd been talking about.

'I hope you like them,' Drakon said as she continued to stare at it all in silence.

Lucy forced herself to say something dutiful which wouldn't sound ungrateful, because there was no denying he must have gone to a lot of trouble. 'They're gorgeous. Did you—?'

'Actually, my partner chose them.'

'Your partner?' she questioned blankly and, although it was unconscious sexism on her part, she instantly imagined some strapping Greek male walking into a store waving a charge card.

'Amy,' he supplied, clearly oblivious to the sudden uncertainty in her voice. 'We've worked together for years.'

She wondered if he was aware of the emotional impact of his words, or of the exact way he'd phrased them—because didn't his relationship with his partner sound way more intimate and close than the one he had with *her*? Lucy could feel her heart punching against her chest in a way which was making her feel almost dizzy. 'I see. And does… Amy choose all your girlfriends' clothes for you?'

'Never. But then I've never been in a situation like this before. I knew your wardrobe was insufficiently versatile to be able to cope with your new role as my wife,' he said, clearly seeking diplomatic words to take the sting out of his statement. 'And I thought you'd be too busy packing to have the time to hit the shops.'

Was that so? Or just that he thought she would fail miserably at the task? That her lack of experience—and money—meant she'd be incapable of selecting her own clothes? But Lucy tried to be positive and take Drakon at his word. She had to be, or this simply wasn't going to work. And she would never have chosen any of these exquisite clothes—not in a million years. She wouldn't have dared purchase items which individually probably cost more than she earned in a month. The question was whether she'd be able to change or return any without embarrassment if they turned out not to fit.

On a nearby chest she could see a deep drawer which was partially open and, sucking in a breath, she walked over and pulled it wide open to find it filled with the most provocative lingerie imaginable. Sexy thong panties were lined up beside balcony bras. Silk stockings and lacy suspender belts lay side by side and Lucy blinked at them in disbelief, sudden ice rippling down her spine. 'Please don't tell me your partner choose *these*?'

He shook his head and laughed. 'Of course not. I bought these myself. It happens to be the most enjoyable shopping trip I've done in years, if you must know. Do you like them?'

Lucy continued to stare at them as she considered his question. On the one hand, of course she did. This was the kind of underwear she'd never imagined herself wearing, not in her wildest dreams. It was impossible not to like such exquisitely made garments, nor to imagine the amount of work which must have gone into making them, but... She turned to him, blinking her eyes rapidly. 'How on earth did you know my size?'

He shrugged. 'I guessed.'

'You guessed,' she repeated slowly. 'Because you have such a comprehensive knowledge of a woman's body that you instinctively know what size bra she wears?'

'I'm in the ship-building industry, Lucy. Learning about dimensions comes with the territory.' A smile curved the edges of his sensual mouth. 'The shoes were a little more difficult.'

'The shoes?' she questioned blankly as the expansive wave of his hand indicated rows of high-heeled shoes and butter-soft leather boots she hadn't even noticed before. She wondered what on earth he was doing as he bent down to retrieve something from underneath the bed, and was momentarily taken aback when he produced a suede moccasin and waved it in the air—like a magician plucking a rabbit from a top hat. 'That's my shoe!' she declared.

'I know.' He gave slow smile. 'I picked it up from that pile by your front door so I could get your size right, on the day I asked you to marry me. It isn't really a winter shoe, so I didn't think you'd notice it had gone.'

It took a couple of seconds before Lucy could bring herself to speak and when she did her words came spitting out like bullets.

'I *did* notice, as it happens. I don't actually own enough pairs of shoes not to realise when one goes missing.' She glared at him, still not quite believing what he'd just told her. 'So let me get this straight. You thought you'd go ahead with some modern-day enactment of Cinderella's slipper and I'm supposed to coo with delight in response?'

'I certainly had hoped for something a little more enthusiastic than your current reaction,' he offered drily.

'Well, please don't bother in future. Like I said, I'm not the biggest fan of surprises. In fact, don't bother with—'

But her sentence was destined never to be completed because Drakon had pulled her into his arms and was kissing her. Kissing her so thoroughly that all the breath left her lungs. And Lucy let him. No, that wasn't quite true. She actively encouraged him. Was it lack of oxygen which made her so instantly yielding? Which made her gasp out a note of breathless approval as his mouth roved hungrily over hers, before darting her tongue into his mouth as if it were a weapon? Or was it simply that she was so *incensed* by what he'd done—by his arrogance and control—that she felt as if she'd been taken over by a different kind of desire? So that very quickly the kiss became something it had never been on Prasinisos. This wasn't soft and searching but punishing, and hard. It was driven by frustration—that he had been so high-handed about overhauling her appearance and given someone she'd never met *carte blanche* to play such a key role in changing it. But there was physical frustration, too, gnawing away inside her like some alien creature she had no idea how to handle. She wondered if sex would release some of the tight frustration which was coiling inside her like a compressed spring. Whether now was the time to tell him she didn't want his *partner* buying her clothes for her. That she wasn't just some kind of doll who could be dressed up for his approval before she was permitted to be seen in public.

'I don't know why we're fighting about clothes, Lucy,' he said unevenly as they broke away to drag oxygen into their air-starved lungs. 'Since my expressed preference is to see you not wearing anything at all.'

And wasn't it pathetic how thrilled she was to hear that husky compliment? As if she was only just beginning to realise that, despite her somewhat homely appearance and complete lack of fashion sense, Drakon Konstantinou really *did* fancy her. But that was one of the reasons she was here, Lucy reminded herself. Her midwifery training wouldn't mean a thing without the white-hot chemistry which seemed to combust whenever they touched.

She felt blindsided by the sense of something which, having been awoken, now needed urgently to be fed. Was that why she let him kiss her again and to deepen it with provocative intimacy, so that she moaned softly into his mouth? And something about that moan made him lever her up against the wall, his face dark and inscrutable as he looked down at her. She could sense the tension which was making his powerful body seem as tight as a strung bow and, where they were touching, her skin felt as if it were on fire.

His fingers were unbuttoning her grey coat and unashamedly roving beneath her sweater and when he jutted his hips forward like that, she could feel the hard column of his erection pressing against her. Beneath her thick denim jeans the molten slick of desire made itself known and Lucy longed for him to touch her there. His fingers were whispering over the cool skin of her torso, moving down towards the top button of her jeans, and she shivered as he popped it open then slid her zip down with a dexterity which suggested he must have undressed millions of women before.

But suddenly Lucy saw herself as an outside observer might see her—all windswept and rumpled with the Greek tycoon's fingers burrowing their way inexorably towards her panties. Why, she hadn't even taken her coat off! She'd only been in his apartment for ten minutes and all they'd done was to fight and kiss and now he was about to take it one step further. If she didn't put a halt to this then before she knew it, she would be pressed up against that wall with Drakon thrusting deep inside her.

She pressed her hand against his chest, feeling the powerful pound of his heart beneath her palm. 'We need to stop this right now.'

'Oh, Lucy. That's not the message I was getting a moment ago,' he drawled.

Well, it's the m-message you're getting now,' she said, unable to iron the tremble from her voice. 'I need to freshen up before Sofia comes back with the baby and to...'

'To what?' he questioned mockingly as her words tailed off.

Lips pressed together, she gave him a determined smile. 'To unpack my case and settle in. And to be honest, Drakon...' She hesitated. 'I think you're right about having separate rooms, but let's do it properly, shall we—with no sneaking around the corridors at midnight? Maybe we *should* wait until we're married until we have..."

'Sex?' he supplied, his eyebrows arching in disbelief. 'Is that what you're trying to say?'

She could feel hot colour flooding her cheeks and, although she realised she could be accused of having double standards, wasn't it better this way? Because what if her earlier doubts came true and she drove him crazy—wouldn't it be easier to draw a line under the whole thing if they *hadn't* become lovers? Easier to walk away if she hadn't had a second distracting taste of physical intimacy? And it would do Drakon good to demonstrate that he wasn't the one making all the rules, and she wasn't going to be totally submissive. To show him that she might have agreed to this marriage of convenience but that didn't make her into some sort of *puppet*.

'That's exactly what I'm trying to say,' she agreed primly.

Still he waited, as if she was going to suddenly turn around and tell him she was joking—as if no woman in her right mind would refuse the opportunity to fall into bed with him at the earliest opportunity.

And Lucy wouldn't have been human if she hadn't enjoyed the brief look of disbelief which flashed from Drakon's ebony eyes when he realised she meant every word she said.

CHAPTER FOUR

LUCY AWOKE TO the sound of a baby's cry and instinct made her sit bolt upright in bed, her heart clenching with painful recognition. Hunger, she thought, as she listened some more. Funny how you could still recognise the different nuances of an infant's cry even though it had been so long since that sound had been part of her daily routine.

Heavy-eyed after a restless night, she got out of bed and it took a few seconds for her befuddled brain to realise she wasn't tucked up in her cosy riverside cottage, but in the fanciest bedroom she'd ever seen. Her new home. The vast Mayfair apartment where she would live as wife to one of the world's most powerful men. Above her head, a chandelier glittered like a shoal of falling diamonds and silk rugs lay strewn over a pale wooden floor, which felt deliciously silky against her bare feet. Grabbing her dressing gown, she knotted it tightly around her waist. It was actually her old dressing gown which she'd brought with her from home because it seemed that her luxury replacement wardrobe didn't cater for a sensible garment you could throw on first thing in the morning to cover up your pyjamas and feed a baby in. *Presumably because once she was married she would no longer be wearing pyjamas.* Running her fingers through her hair to tame its tousled wildness, she set off towards the nursery.

The crying had stopped by the time Lucy got there and she was greeted by a scene of perfect domesticity. Sofia was sitting on a yellow sofa giving Xander a bottle while soft nursery rhymes played gently in the background. It felt a little strange for Lucy to be standing in her nightclothes in front of someone she'd only met a couple of times but the middle-aged nanny merely looked up and gave her a friendly smile as she entered the room.

'Good morning, Lucy,' she said. 'Did you sleep well?'

'Very well, thank you,' said Lucy with more politeness than truth—because nothing was more boring than hearing someone relate the story of what a bad night they'd had. She certainly didn't want Sofia quizzing her about the reasons for her restlessness. *Reason,* she corrected herself silently. One reason alone—all six feet three of him. 'You should have woken me.'

Sofia shook her head. 'Drakon said you were to be left undisturbed.'

Drakon. Lucy started at the mention of his name and she thought—how pathetic is *that*? Had her heart missed a beat because she'd resisted his sexual overtures when she'd arrived yesterday and been haunted by tantalising dreams about him ever since? Or because it was still difficult to believe that the gorgeous billionaire would soon be her husband and that this was now her reality? A reality brought home by the stilted dinner they'd shared last evening, presided over by his stern-faced housekeeper, Zena—a meal which had kept being interrupted while Drakon had dealt with one international phone call after another. He'd been talking to someone in New York when eventually Lucy had excused herself and his absent wave of farewell as she'd headed off to her bedroom had spoken volumes. He hadn't followed her and she hadn't really expected him to, because instinct told her that a man like Drakon would never beg a woman for intimacy when she had told him it wasn't going to happen. She'd lain there listening until eventually she'd heard him heading for bed, freezing with hope and expectation as his footsteps had paused outside her door, before moving on. As an introduction to life in the fast lane, it hadn't exactly felt welcoming. Or maybe he had just been making a point…

She stood in the doorway watching as Sofia fed the baby and suddenly felt almost redundant. With a touch of anxiety she licked her lips and looked around, but the room was pristinely tidy. 'Is there anything I can do? Some dusting, or tidying up?'

'No, honestly, I'm fine. It's all under control. Drakon employs an army of people to do the housework for him. He's going down for a nap shortly but you could do the midday feed if you like. But only if you have time before you go out for lunch,' Sofia amended hastily.

Lucy maintained her bright smile even though she was aware that her voice sounded brittle. 'I wasn't aware that I *was* going out for lunch.'

Sofia's eyes crinkled in a smile. 'Apparently. Zena told me. The car has been ordered for you. Lucky you,' she added, in her perfect but heavily accented English. 'It will inevitably be somewhere grand.'

Lucy hoped her expression didn't give away her feelings as she returned to her bedroom and tugged off her dressing gown. Whether or not the restaurant was grand was completely beside the point. It was one thing to agree to a marriage of convenience, she thought furiously as she stood beneath the fierce blast of the shower. But quite another when she was being treated a convenience. Did Drakon think he could just move her around like a vacuum cleaner? How come the housekeeper and the nanny knew she was going out for lunch, when it was a mystery to her?

She dried her hair and, for the first time, tried on some of the new clothes which had been chosen by his business partner, Amy. Last night at dinner she'd stubbornly insisted on wearing one of her own dresses, still needled by the fact that Drakon had asked someone else to kit her out for her new role in his life. Yet hadn't her defiance backfired on her, so that she'd been left having to endure the entire meal feeling somewhat *less than*? Her navy shirt-dress dress was her go-to favourite but there was no doubt that the fabric looked cheap against all the unrestrained luxury of Drakon's home and Lucy was certain his housekeeper had been looking down her nose at her, as if wondering why someone like her was associating with the impeccably clad tycoon. Hadn't the same question crossed her own mind more than once as the evening had progressed?

So just go with the flow, she told herself as she rifled through the colour-coordinated rows of garments before pulling out a long-sleeved dress in silk chiffon. The soft violet hue was the colour which sometimes tinged a late sunset and, admittedly, a shade she would never have thought of choosing for herself. The delicate fabric floated to just above the knee and made her waist look positively *tiny*, and she teamed it with a pair of shoes higher than anything she'd ever worn before. Did the added height make her assume a rather awkward gait? Was that why the middle-aged housekeeper did a double-take as Lucy cautiously picked her way into the dining room for breakfast?

'Good morning, Dhespinis Phillips,' said Zena.

'Good morning, Zena.' Lucy sat down at

the table and gave the housekeeper a nervous smile. 'Um…is Drakon…?'

'The master went to the office at seven this morning, but he left you a note,' said Zena, indicating an envelope which was propped up in front of a vase of flame-coloured roses. 'I will bring you some breakfast.'

'Thank you.'

Lucy thought about the housekeeper's words as she picked up the envelope. The master. It was an oddly archaic term of address yet it seemed scarily suitable. Because Drakon *was* the master, wasn't he? The master of all he surveyed. At least that was the impression he gave, with his cabal of loyal staff, his enormous wealth and his different homes dotted around the world. Was he expecting to become *her* master once they were wed— was she to obey him in all things, as the marriage ceremony used to demand but which most modern couples now rejected? And shouldn't this be something they discussed before she allowed him to slide that gold ring on her finger?

Slitting open the envelope, she pulled out a single sheet of paper, realising that this was the first time she'd ever seen Drakon's writing. It was exactly as she would have imagined it to be. Angular black lines slashed over the thick writing paper. Succinct, forceful and strong. A reluctant smile curved the edges of her lips. Just like him.

My car will pick you up at 12.25. We'll eat lunch at the Granchester for reasons which will quickly become evident.

Mysterious as well as autocratic, she thought as she drank some inky Greek coffee and picked at a bowl of iced mango, before getting up to leave.

She spent the next hour exploring the sprawling apartment and studying some of the books she found in the library, before going to the nursery to give the baby his feed. But at least her interaction with Xander cheered her, and as he glugged greedily on the teat she buried her nose in his silky hair, remembering how much she loved tiny babies and how much she'd missed them. And this baby would soon be her *son*. The child she had always longed for and never thought she'd have.

But she couldn't stem the dark doubts which began to crowd into her mind as she winded the infant and laid him in his crib. He was so cute, with his black eyes and matching hair—a miniature version of his father's identical twin brother. What if she fell hopelessly in love with this little infant and her marriage failed, as so many marriages did, despite Drakon's determination for that not to happen? Because he couldn't control everything, could he, no matter how much he tried?

He'd told her he didn't believe in love and that he'd never been in love—but who was to say that the thunderbolt wouldn't one day hit him, as it had hit so many cynical disbelievers in the past? In that scenario, wouldn't she become an also-ran in Xander's life? The woman with no blood ties with no real claim on the child who could be dispensed of as carelessly as you would yesterday's newspapers. Lucy sighed, knowing she mustn't think like that because nobody was ever given any guarantees in this life—you just had to do the best you could in the circumstances.

She was nervous as she snuggled herself into the cashmere coat with the velvet collar and slid into the back of the waiting limousine, and even more nervous when the car drew up outside the landmark Granchester Hotel after a ridiculously short journey from the apartment. Outside the impressive

building, she could see an enormous Christmas tree, topped with a huge golden star and
smaller gold and silver stars which dangled
from the abundant branches. The doorman
hurried forward to open the door for her and
Lucy gingerly made her way into the gilded
foyer in her new shoes, her heart missing a
beat when she spotted Drakon, with his back
to her, standing beside another decorated fir
tree—almost as big as the one at the front of
the hotel.

Dark, broad-shouldered and powerful, he
seemed oblivious to the stares he was attract-
ing from the other guests and she wondered
whether something must have alerted him
to her approach. Why else did he suddenly
turn around? He was mid-conversation on his
phone but his eyes narrowed and his words
seemed to die away as she approached and,
abruptly, he cut the call. Something about the
way he was looking at her was making her
feel breathless and excited and scared all at
the same time and Lucy found herself resent-
ing his effortless power over her.

'Lucy,' he murmured as he helped her slide
the coat from her shoulders. 'You're here.'

'Yes, I'm here. Though I could have walked
in less time than it took to drive!'

'I don't think so. Not in those shoes,' he commented wryly, his gaze travelling down to her feet and lingering on them for longer than was strictly necessary.

'You don't like them?' she asked, berating herself for needing reassurance but asking for it all the same.

Drakon heard the genuine doubt in her voice and, unusually, he was surprised—searching her face for signs of disingenuousness and finding none. Was she out of her mind? Didn't she realise that every man in the place was staring at her as if she'd just tumbled down from the heavens? Of course, she didn't. Because she was totally without guile, he realised. An innocent who stood out from the women he usually mixed with. But she looked *incredible*. Having slipped the coat from her shoulders, he saw the filmy dress, which hinted at the firm flesh which lay beneath, and in those spike-heeled shoes... He swallowed. Didn't her calves look ripe for stroking and her ankles made for wrapping around a man's neck?

'I like them very much,' he said unevenly. 'In fact, there's a term which is commonly used to describe shoes like those but I don't think that now is the right time to introduce it into the conversation.'

Predictably, she blushed and Drakon felt a powerful beat of lust, which made him wonder why he'd arranged to meet her here, in one of the most public venues in the city, rather than exploiting the intimacy of his nearby apartment. *You know why,* he thought grimly. Because she had firmly stated that they weren't going to have sex until they were married and he was in no doubt that she meant it. Just as he was aware that he was in part responsible for her old-fashioned stance.

He frowned. He'd thought he'd tantalise her by offering her a separate room, thinking that *interludes* of pleasure would keep her on her toes. More than that, he liked his own space and was used to it because he'd never shared a bedroom full-time with a woman before. He'd thought he would use the opportunity for some extended personal space before things changed once they were married.

Yet Lucy had neatly turned the tables on him by telling him she thought they should wait until after the wedding before being intimate again. He sighed with frustration and anticipation—tinged with a grudging sense of admiration, because he couldn't think of another woman who would have refused to have sex with him.

And if that was the way she wanted to play it, why not go along with it? He had chosen her because of her pliability but the fact that she was now showing some token resistance made this arranged marriage of theirs seem a little less predictable. In a way, it amused him to let Lucy Phillips think she was calling the shots, because he could have broken her self-imposed sexual embargo any time he wanted. He knew that and he suspected she knew it, too.

The pupils of her eyes were huge and dark and he could sense the sudden tension in her body as she met his gaze, as if silently acknowledging the inexplicable chemistry which was sparking between them. He'd never seen her looking so sleek and so sexy. He'd never imagined she would scrub up this well. The tremble of her lips kick-started something indefinable inside him and a lump rose in his throat. Drakon swallowed, certain that if he reached out to whisper his fingertips over the pulse which fluttered so wildly at the base of her neck, or snaked his hand around her impossibly slender waist, she would do the predictable thing, and melt against him with a hunger which matched his.

But leaving aside the fact they were in a public space, it would be wrong to act on hormonal impulse. He would use restraint because this was too important a deal to jeopardise with sexual impatience. And if he was being honest, wasn't it turning him on to an unbearable pitch at the thought of being made to wait—he who'd never had to wait for a woman in his life? True, she might be playing games with him—possibly in an attempt to make him fall in love with her—but that certainly wasn't going to give him any sleepless nights. She would soon discover he was immune to the ruses women employed and was not in the market for 'love'. All he cared about was that Lucy Phillips was going to make the perfect mother to his adopted son and the exquisite sharpening of his sexual appetite in the meantime was simply a bonus.

Touching his fingers to her back, he guided her towards the Garden Room restaurant. 'Come on. Let's go and have lunch.'

They walked along a long corridor, where golden baubles and scarlet ribbons were woven into the seasonal greenery which festooned the walls, and he watched as she looked around and drank it all in.

'What an amazing hotel,' she exclaimed. 'It's enormous!'

'You've never been here before?'

'Funny you should say that, but no,' she answered, dead-pan. 'Five-star hotels aren't my usual stomping ground on one of my rare visits to the capital. I've seen photos of it, obviously.'

'I thought we could get married here,' he offered casually.

'Here?' she said, coming to an abrupt halt just before they reached the restaurant entrance and nearly losing her balance on the spike-heeled shoes.

'You really don't like surprises, do you?' He put out an arm to steady her. 'Why shouldn't we? It's a very famous wedding venue.'

'I know it is! Don't film stars and princes choose it for their nuptials?'

'I don't keep tabs on celebrity weddings unless I happen to be a guest at them,' he drawled. 'But Zac Constantinides, the owner, is a friend of mine, so he's given us a date when it was supposed to be shut. As a favour, you understand.'

'Of course,' she said faintly.

'It's a perfect solution, especially this close to Christmas. So what do you say, Lucy? Apparently, there's an in-house wedding planner who'll do most of the donkey work for you.'

Lucy registered his puzzled expression as she hesitated. Was he expecting her to gush her thanks, or swoon about the sumptuousness of the venue, instead of standing there chewing her lip in a state of nervous anxiety? But she was having difficulty getting her head round the idea of someone like her standing up in a place this grand and making her wedding vows.

But what was the alternative? Surely she could overcome her nerves enough to get married in one of the world's most glamorous venues—especially if she was marrying such a high-profile man. And wouldn't the wedding co-ordinator take away some of the stress?

'You had something else in mind?' he prompted, when still she said nothing.

Lucy shook her head. 'You don't mind the fact that it will be a very *public* wedding?'

'You think I want to hide the fact away? I'm Greek, Lucy,' he said simply. 'And we Greeks like a good party.'

'Okay,' she said, speaking as quietly as

possible in order to eliminate any telltale tremble of nerves. 'In that case—why not?'

'Not the most rapturous reaction I might have hoped for,' he observed drily. 'But I suppose it will have to do. Come on. Let's eat.'

The maître d' greeted him with easy familiarity as he showed them to a table which offered a perfect view of the winter garden, with its icy fountain and dark red branches of dogwood.

'Are we celebrating anything in particular today, Mr Konstantinou?'

'We certainly are. Ask the sommelier to bring my fiancée a glass of Dom Perignon rosé, would you, please, Carlos?'

There was a split-second pause and, when he spoke, Carlos's voice sounded faintly strangulated. 'Certainly, sir. And for yourself?'

'Just water, thanks.'

Lucy waited until they were alone before she spoke. 'That man looked as if he'd just been hit by a sledgehammer when you described me as your fiancée.'

'He was probably surprised, *neh*. I have a reputation which precedes me.'

'What kind of reputation?'

He gave a wolfish smile. 'As a man who has never wanted to settle down. A man who was fundamentally opposed to marriage. Maybe I was unconsciously drawing a line in the sand, to demonstrate that, from now on, things are going to be very different.'

Were they? Lucy wondered distractedly. But how different? A glass of champagne was placed in front of her but she stared uninterestedly at the fizzing pink bubbles before lifting her eyes to Drakon. 'I suppose you've brought loads of women to this hotel in the past? Probably to have lunch in this very restaurant before taking them to bed?'

His black gaze was very steady. 'I'm not going to lie to you, Lucy. I was never promiscuous or indiscriminate but I'm thirty-one, single and, yes, of course I've slept with women during that time. Why wouldn't I? The evidence is everywhere if you care to look for it—because you can find out pretty much anything online.' He leaned forward, across the starched linen of the tablecloth. 'But I'm hoping you won't bother because I'm being perfectly transparent with you. I see no point in pretending to you, or rewriting history. You may have been a virgin when we hooked up, but I most certainly was not.'

'So why announce our engagement to

someone you don't really know? Was that really necessary?'

'I think so. Carlos is perfectly aware how these things work.' He gave a flicker of a smile. 'He'll mention it to someone, who'll mention it to someone else. The press will get to hear about it and there will be a diary piece—only by then it will be old news.' There was a brief pause. 'Like I said, it draws a line in the sand and discourages any hopeful overtures from ex-lovers.'

His statement was more matter-of-fact than arrogant and Lucy told herself it shouldn't have bothered her, but it did, and she was taken aback by the hot flash of jealousy which pulsed through her. But of *course* he would have plenty of exes eager to return into his life. Hadn't she been pretty keen to see him herself when she'd returned from Prasinisos, forever glancing at her mobile phone and wondering if he would ring? Which, of course, he hadn't.

And that was what she needed to remember. The one fact which should never be far from her mind. That she would never have seen Drakon Konstantinou again if his brother and sister-in-law hadn't decided to go on a narcotic-fuelled bender and leave their baby son with no parents.

'Did Xander have any other relatives?' she asked suddenly. 'Apart from his mother?'

He shook his head. 'I put an investigator on the case. Niko's wife was adopted as a baby, but had been estranged from her family for many years. There were no living blood relatives, so Xander will have no connection with the past.' His expression grew shuttered. 'And it will be better for him in the long run. Much better.'

'In your opinion.'

'It's my opinion which counts,' he said cuttingly. 'And what I say goes. And I'd rather my adoptive son wasn't in the grip of people I don't know. People who might influence him to follow the same sorry path as his parents.'

Feeling faint, Lucy gripped the stem of her champagne flute, but she didn't lift it to her lips. She was afraid that her hands would tremble too much and she would spill it all over the perfectly starched tablecloth. Because it wasn't just the things Drakon had said which freaked her out, but the way he'd said them. He'd sounded so...*ruthless*. As if you could take the parts of somebody's life which you didn't like and simply wipe them out—like airbrushing a photo or altering something on your camera phone. But if he'd sounded ruthless it was because he *was*, she reminded herself. She should forget that at her peril. Suddenly she was glad that she was going to be there for baby Xander. Glad she would be able to fight his corner, because surely he needed someone there for him when Drakon started being even more high-handed than usual.

Eventually she felt calm enough to take a sip of wine, which eased some of her tension, and beneath the table she stretched out her legs, her new pointy shoes touching what she thought was the leg of the table, but Drakon's mocking eyes informed her that she'd made direct contact with his calf. Hastily, she jerked her foot away and his gaze grew more thoughtful.

'So why don't you like surprises?' he asked suddenly.

It was a question she hadn't been expecting, and if she hadn't been so blindsided by everything which had happened in the last twenty-four hours Lucy might have glossed over it—because why revisit pain when you didn't have to? But Drakon seemed to have an uncanny knack of getting her to open up.

He'd done it on the night of the school reunion and he was doing it again now. She wondered if it was because he'd known her so long ago, in those days when she'd had a mother and a brother and hadn't been such a lost soul. And surely if they were planning on spending the rest of their lives together, he needed to know some of the things which made her tick. Only some of them, mind. A twist of guilt seared her heart and she stared down at her fingernails before looking up to meet the searching gleam of his eyes. 'I guess I just associate surprises with unpleasant things.'

'What kind of things?'

'Oh, you know.' She shrugged her shoulders restlessly. 'All the stuff which comes with having family in the military. The heavy knock at the door, or the ring of the telephone late at night. The men in uniform who stand on your doorstep with grim faces as they prepare to give you the news.' News which rocked the foundations of your world and made you realise nothing was ever going to be the same again. Yet hadn't it been those experiences that had provided the lessons which had enabled Lucy to ring-fence her emotions and keep herself safe from pain? Which had forced her to build barriers around her heart so she could never be hurt like that again? She folded her lips together. Wasn't that one of the *good* things about agreeing to marry a man like Drakon—that he had spelt out he didn't do love either? He had his own emotional barriers in place and that made them equal in a totally unexpected way. He could never hurt her because she would never let him get that close.

And the bottom line was that he didn't want to get close.

'That must have been tough,' he observed.

'Life is tough, Drakon—as I'm sure Xander would tell us if he were able to speak.'

He nodded, his eyes still searching her face, as if he was seeing something he hadn't noticed before. 'I don't want any more children,' he said suddenly.

'I'm sorry?'

'More kids.' His voice was rough. 'One is my limit and if you want more—'

'I don't,' she said quickly, as relief washed over her. 'I think children should only ever be conceived in love and we've both agreed that isn't what is driving this marriage of ours.'

His nodded slowly, his eyes narrowing. 'There's something else we haven't addressed,' he said softly.

Her brow creased. 'Which is?'

'The ring.'

'The ring?' she repeated.

'An engagement ring. It's fairly traditional in most cultures, as far as I'm aware. Surely you must have been expecting one, Lucy? I thought all women had preferences about what kind of jewels they'd like in this situation.'

'No, Drakon, all women do not—at least, not those of us who live relatively normal lives. I have better things to do with my time than drool about diamonds.' Recklessly, she took another mouthful of champagne— a much bigger one this time—which really went to her head. *Serves you right,* she thought dazedly as she carefully replaced the glass on the table. 'I'm astonished you didn't ask your partner, Amy, to select one for me as she did my clothes,' she said, in an acid tone she'd never heard herself use before. 'Or maybe she already has?'

He shook his head. 'The answer is no on both counts. She couldn't have done even if I wanted her to because she's flown out to Singapore on business.'

'Gosh. How will you be able to manage without her?' she questioned, the lingering effects of the wine still evident in her unusually flippant tone.

'Amy's absence certainly makes me realise how hard she works.' Almost carelessly, he slid a small box across the table. 'I bought this for you myself, so if you don't like it you're at liberty to change it.' As Lucy continued to stare at it, he lowered his voice into a murmured command. 'Stop looking at it as though it were an unexploded bomb. Open it.'

With faltering fingers she did just that, and it was a measure of just how glitzy the world in which she now found herself that Lucy realised she was expecting to see a whacking great diamond, or an emerald the size of a gull's egg. Because wasn't that what billionaires usually bought for their future brides, especially if it was an arranged marriage? Some huge chunk of glittering gemstone which would be way too big for her finger and look like paste on someone so unremittingly ordinary.

But as she flipped open the box to reveal a ring, it was to discover that Drakon had surprised her and in a way she almost wished he hadn't, because it made her feel quite breathless. Set in embellished gold was a square-cut sapphire the indefinable colour of a spot of ink dropped into a beaker of water, which glittered in the pale winter light that streamed in through the windows. It was delicate, unusual and beautiful. The most beautiful ring she had ever seen.

'What made you choose this?' she questioned shakily.

He shrugged. 'The jeweller asked me what colour your eyes were.'

Lucy's heart raced and a strange, restrictive dryness in her throat made it difficult for her to speak as for one split second she allowed herself to sink into a fantasy of longing. 'And you remembered?'

'It's hardly neuroscience, Lucy. I only saw you a couple of days ago.' His slightly impatient look was followed by a dismissive shake of his head as he picked up his menu. 'Come on. Let's order. I have a meeting this afternoon.'

CHAPTER FIVE

STANDING IN ALL her wedding finery and trying not to let her nerves get the better of her, Lucy waited in the anteroom of the grand ballroom where her marriage to Drakon was about to take place. Tightly, she gripped her bouquet, which contrasted so vividly with the snowy whiteness of her dress. Scarlet roses flared like beacons amid the lush greenery and a sprig of mistletoe had been playfully added at the last minute by the Granchester's in-house florist, as a nod towards the fact that it was almost Christmas.

Donna, the wedding planner, had arranged for carols to be piped through the hotel's sophisticated sound system because 'everyone loves Christmas carols'. But if the seasonal songs were supposed to be soothing or comforting then they had failed in their mission because Lucy's brow was clammy and her heart was racing beneath the heavily embellished dress which she'd been persuaded into against her better judgment. She'd wanted something simple. Something plain, in ivory—an outfit she didn't have to think about, rather than something which would wear *her*. But the dress designer had explained that a room as grand as the Granchester ballroom needed a gown to stand out among all the lavish fixtures and fittings. Something which would fill the makeshift aisle rather than getting completely lost in it. Which was why she was wearing jewel-encrusted white silk satin, with an oversized veil cascading down her back, looking as if a tipper truck had just offloaded a ton of sequin-sprinkled meringue.

Her throat felt like dust and her lips were dry and she kept thinking, *Surely this isn't how a bride is supposed to feel?* Lost and displaced and alone. Wondering what she'd let herself in for and whether she'd been a fool to accept the Greek magnate's offer of marriage. But how did she *expect* to feel, when the hectic preparations for the imminent ceremony seemed to have done nothing but emphasise the huge differences between her and her billionaire bridegroom? Especially since, after citing a busy work schedule, Drakon had absented himself from all the arrangements—except for providing a list of guests he wished to be invited, which hugely outnumbered her own.

'So it's definitely just *five* guests on your side?' The wedding planner had clearly been puzzled as she'd looked at Lucy expectantly, as if waiting to be told there'd been an elemental mix-up in the numbers and she'd missed off a nought.

Lucy's smile had stayed firmly in place. 'That's right.'

'Okay… Well, if you're *quite* sure…'

She supposed it wasn't conventional for the bride to be so sparsely represented but Lucy had been strong in her determination only to have people there who meant something to her. Wasn't this wedding fake enough already without her shipping in a load of guests just for show? Her parents and brother were dead and her only other living relative was Auntie Alice, who lived in Australia and had been unable to make the wedding this close to the holidays. And it wasn't as if she and Drakon had already formed lots of friends between them as a couple, was it? They'd barely spent more than a couple of hours together at a time during the frantic run-up to the big day.

And whose fault was that?

Hers and hers alone. Her determination to keep their sleeping arrangements separate until after the ceremony had given Drakon free rein to throw himself into his work and he had been out at the office from dawn to dusk. Why, he hadn't even asked her a single question about what they'd be eating at the wedding breakfast!

Caroline, her boss from Caro's Canapés, was going to be in attendance—as well as two of the other waitresses, Judii and Jade. A heavily pregnant Patti, her best friend from midwifery days, was also going to be there—along with Tom, her new husband. And they all loved her, Lucy reminded herself fiercely. They would be rooting for her even if her sudden decision to marry a man they'd never heard her mention had perplexed them. She didn't even have anyone to give her away, but had been loath to go searching for someone suitable. Tom had kindly offered to step in but Lucy barely knew her best friend's husband. Which was why she would be walking towards Drakon completely on her own.

Donna stuck her head round the door and gave her a thumbs up. 'Ready?'

Lucy touched her fingers to the pale glittery veil which rippled down her back, and nodded. She just needed to remember the special Greek traditions she'd been taught and which were to be incorporated into the day. They would eat sugared almonds at some point and people would attempt to pin money to her dress. After their wedding rings had been blessed, they would be placed on their fingers three times—to symbolise the unity of their entwined lives.

And during all this she would try her best not to feel like a hypocrite.

'I'm ready,' she whispered.

The double doors were opened with a flourish and all Lucy could see was the long walk which lay ahead, decked on either side by chairs festooned with yet more greenery and slivers of golden ribbon. Everyone turned to look at her and she clutched her bouquet even tighter, aware that even in here Donna had gone over the top with the Christmas theme, but she hadn't wanted to come over as some sort of Grinch by telling her not to bother. Yet somehow the gloriousness of the occasion was starting to feel overwhelmingly poignant.

Tall candles of scarlet flickered patterns of transparent gold onto the gilded walls and silver stars dangled on spangled strings which hung from the vaulted ceiling. The sound of a carol being sung by a single boy's voice in Greek was making Lucy want to blink her eyes against the unwanted threat of tears and she hoped she didn't need to blow her nose during the service because she didn't have a handkerchief.

And there was Xander, fast asleep in the arms of his nanny, Sofia. Darling little Xander, whom she'd fed and played with that morning before she'd left for the hotel, wondering if Drakon ever intended to be anything other than a father in name. Because the man who was supremely confident in all things seemed wary of the innocent child he had adopted. She could count on the fingers of one hand the times she'd seen him hold the baby and she'd found herself wondering if she should try to bridge the distance he seemed to have constructed between himself and Xander. Was it her place to even try?

She began to walk with small steps—partly because she was terrified of toppling over in her spiky heels, but also in an attempt to quell her spiralling nerves as she saw her

Greek bridegroom standing beneath an arch of Christmas roses.

As the music heralded her arrival, he didn't turn to look at her and although Lucy told herself it was easier not to have to face the enigmatic glitter of his eyes, it was also daunting to be confronted by his imposing back view. She gazed at his powerful body, clad in a dark suit which accentuated his broad shoulders and muscular limbs. A body which very soon...

No. She wasn't going to fret about her wedding night or give into the nebulous fears which had been bugging her. She wasn't going to start worrying that their time on Prasinisos had been an aberration—a peculiar one-off, fuelled by sunshine and novelty.

Because what if she disappointed her new husband on the first night of their honeymoon? What if the reality of an arranged marriage had somehow extinguished the passion they'd shared before? Wasn't that another reason why she had been secretly relieved to maintain separate rooms until the wedding—because she'd been afraid of being put to the test, and failing?

At long last she reached the fragrant green arch and Drakon turned around and stared down at her. He took her trembling hand in his and suddenly this became about much more than whether this was the craziest thing she had ever done. Suddenly Lucy felt breathless with longing as Drakon's strength seemed to radiate from his powerful frame, his black eyes crinkling in a way which reminded her how long she'd known him. Surely that counted for something. Surely they could make this work if they worked at it.

'Okay?' he mouthed.

She gave a quick nod. 'I think so.'

'You look beautiful.'

'Th-thank you.'

Her voice sounded tremulous, Drakon thought as the celebrant began to intone the words. And her face was as white as her dress. He stole another glance at her, aware that his compliment had been dutiful rather than genuine because this dazzling creature didn't look a bit like Lucy. The huge dress swamped her and the sequin-spattered veil did not seem to sit well with the simple country image she'd always projected. And her fingers were cold. As cold as the gold band which, moments later, he slid onto her finger. He looked down at a similar band which now gleamed unfamiliarly against his own olive skin. He'd never worn a ring before and it felt heavy and alien.

'I now pronounce you man and wife.'

The finality of the words shattered his thoughts like a spray gun and Lucy's blue eyes were blank as she looked up at him, almost as if the whole ceremony had happened without her realising it. *You and me both,* agape mou, he thought with a black-humoured sense of identity.

'You may now kiss the bride.'

Drakon slid his arms around her waist and bent towards her, aware that the kiss was mainly for the benefit of the watching congregation. He hadn't kissed her since that afternoon when she'd arrived at his apartment and, as a consequence, his desire for her had reached a level of intensity he'd never experienced before. For days it had been heating his blood and gnawing at his senses with a remorselessness which had left him barely able to think straight. It had tortured him. Tormented him. But hadn't he almost *enjoyed* the boundaries she'd primly put in place, which had heightened his exquisite anticipation of tonight's consummation? Strange to think that this most unlikely candidate was the first woman who had ever denied him anything. Which was why he didn't make this a real kiss. He didn't dare. He was afraid that once he'd started he wouldn't be able to stop. That he would pin her down to the ground and rip that monstrous dress from her body—contemptuously tossing aside the tattered satin to touch the soft flesh beneath. He gave a brief nod as he brushed his lips over hers, in nothing more than a swift acknowledgement that the deal was done and dusted.

But he was aware of the disappointment which flashed through her eyes as he pulled away from her. And something else, too. Something which looked almost like *fear*, as the applause of the assembled guests echoed up into the gilded arches and they walked into an adjoining room to sign the register. Was it the sudden inexplicable need to quell that fear which made him whisper his fingertips against her waist, so that she relaxed a little?

'All done,' he said.

She nodded. 'I guess so.'

'So how does it feel to be Mrs Konstantinou? Kyria Konstantinou,' he amended as they made their way towards the desk, where the registrar was waiting.

'Slightly weird,' she admitted. 'Probably

about as weird as it feels for you to have taken a wife, but no doubt we'll get used to it.'

Her brisk words were reassuring. Drakon had wondered if she would expect him to recite affectionate words he didn't really mean—saccharine statements which would leave him with a bad taste in his mouth. But if she was prepared to treat this marriage as nothing more than a business merger with benefits—what could possibly go wrong?

'I suggest the best way of getting used to it is by having as early a night as possible,' he said smoothly, scrawling his signature on the wedding licence and strangely pleased by the blush which flared in her cheeks. 'Since tomorrow I'm taking you on honeymoon.'

She blinked at him—unaccustomed mascara making her eyes look huge and smoky. 'We're having a honeymoon?'

'Isn't that traditional?' he murmured as his finger trailed over her pearl-encrusted sleeve. 'As traditional as your white gown and veil? You'll enjoy it, Lucy. I thought we'd fly to my island for the Christmas Eve celebrations.'

'You mean Prasinisos?

He smiled. 'At the last count, Prasinisos was the only island I owned.'

She pushed the waterfall of white veil back

over her shoulder. 'I never really thought about going to Greece at Christmas time.'

'You thought my homeland neglected the winter holiday entirely?' he challenged mockingly. 'Or that it only comes to life when you can dip your sun-baked body into the wine-dark sea?' He gave a soft laugh. 'Then you must be prepared to have your mind changed.'

'And what about Xander?' she asked tentatively. 'What's going to happen to our...son?'

Drakon frowned. His son. It was a word he had so far avoided using because it had been strange to think of himself as a parent. It still was. Every time he looked at the helpless infant, he could feel a cold fear clench at his heart, which made him turn away. But while nobody could accuse him of being falsely demonstrative, surely she didn't think him uncaring enough to drag the infant halfway across the world and back for a couple of days? He narrowed his eyes. 'The child's presence is unnecessary,' he said. 'And the journey will be too much.'

'But it's Christmas!'

'And you think a baby of less than three months will miss out on opening his presents?' he demanded.

'Please don't put words in my mouth, Drakon!'

'Then stop being so emotional. We will be gone for just three nights and then we will be back home in Mayfair.'

'It just feels… I don't know… It feels weird to leave him behind.'

'You'll get used to it. That's why we employ a loyal and caring nanny. Now, wipe that frown from your face and let's go and greet our guests. My godfather has travelled here from Honolulu and I really want you to meet him.'

With a heart which felt suddenly heavy, Lucy followed Drakon back into the ballroom to the sound of loud clapping and people crying, *'Opa!'*

Smiling at the guests, she tried to shake off her worries about guilt she'd felt when the celebrant had talked about them extending their family and her gaze had dropped to stare at the gleaming marble floor. But she'd told herself that none of his words were relevant, not in their case—and there was no need to feel guilty. Drakon didn't want any more children, so the fact she was unable to give him any was neither here nor there.

Her heavy train slithering like a giant

white snake behind her, she accompanied her new husband to the far end of the crowded ballroom, where his godfather was holding court. A handsome, silver-haired property magnate in his early sixties, Milo Lazopoulos was charming as he bent to kiss her on each cheek. The adoring crowd around him instantly dispersed, leaving the two men to speak briefly in Greek before Drakon excused himself and disappeared. Putting her bouquet down on a nearby table and finding herself alone with his godfather, Lucy was forced to address Milo's probing line of conversation once the traditional pleasantries had been dispensed with.

'I thank heaven that Drakon has stepped up to the plate and taken on the responsibilities left behind by his brother.' Milo shook his head. 'It was a terrible business. A terrible end to all that golden promise Niko was born with. To lose everything because you want to stick a needle in your arm. I just can't understand it.'

'They say that addiction is an illness,' said Lucy quietly. 'So perhaps we should feel compassion for him.'

Milo's gaze was piercing. 'Drakon tells me you used to be a nurse.'

'That's right.' Lucy nodded. 'A midwife, actually.'

'Which means you are well equipped to take on a young baby,' he observed.

'I'm going to do my very best.' She wondered what else Drakon had told his godfather. That they had agreed to a loveless marriage which was more of a business arrangement than anything else?

'But you left midwifery?' Milo continued.

'Not everyone stays in the job for life,' she commented gently.

'Because it was too distressing?'

There was a pause and Lucy could hear the loud beat of her heart hammering beneath the embellished bodice of her wedding dress. He was insightful, she thought, as well as being blunt. There were distressing aspects in every field of nursing, of course there were. But she wouldn't be telling Milo about her real reason for leaving the profession. Or Drakon, come to think about it. There was no need to, she reminded herself painfully. 'Something like that,' she agreed.

Something about her guarded reply made Milo's eyes narrow. Was he aware of her misgivings and did this make him decide that his interrogation had been a little on the harsh side? 'You seem the perfect choice of wife for my godson, Lucy. Someone calm and solid. A safe harbour after all those years of him resisting all forms of commitment. Funny, we always thought he'd...' His words came to an abrupt halt as he plucked two glasses of champagne from a passing waitress and handed one to Lucy. 'Let me be the first to toast the beautiful bride,' he said, the fine lines which edged his black eyes crinkling into a smile as he held his goblet aloft. *'Na zisoun!'*

But Lucy could be insightful too and as she chinked her glass to his she wondered what he wasn't telling her. 'Always thought he'd, what...?'

She could see speculation flashing in Milo's eyes, as if working out what she would or wouldn't be able to tolerate. But she kept her gaze firm and steady, willing him to tell her the truth. Because this was a marriage based on truth, wasn't it? Not fairy tales or fantasy.

He shrugged. 'We always thought he might marry Amy.'

Lucy nodded, recognising the name immediately. Of course. Amy. Drakon's business partner—and the woman who had bought his prospective bride a wardrobe of beautiful new clothes. The elusive Amy who was currently in Singapore wheeling and dealing and had apparently been unable to make the ceremony. She'd wondered if Amy's explanation of back-to-back meetings had been true, or whether it had been too painful for her to watch Drakon take another woman as his bride. Lucy hoped her expression didn't give her feelings away as insecurity began to pump through her veins. Instead, she aimed for the calmness she'd always been able to project even in the most trying circumstances—and this was hardly up there with those, was it?

'We haven't actually met,' she said, managing to produce a smile from somewhere.

Milo turned his head as there was some sort of commotion over by the double set of gilded doors and a murmur went up around the ballroom. 'Well, I think that's just about to change,' he said.

Lucy followed the direction of his gaze in time to witness the entrance of the most beautiful woman she had ever seen. The rich emerald material of her slinky dress provided a luscious backdrop for the shiny hair which spilled over her narrow shoulders like melted dark chocolate. Her lips were as red as the berries in the garlands of holly and people were crowding around her making spontaneous whoops of joy—their behaviour in marked contrast to the wariness they'd displayed when introduced to Lucy.

Amy's dark eyes were searching the room until they alighted on the bride and Lucy felt her heart give a great lurch as Milo spoke.

'Here's Amy,' he said quietly. 'And she's heading this way.'

CHAPTER SIX

'DON'T LOOK LIKE THAT,' Drakon instructed softly.

'Like what?'

'Like a sacrificial lamb all poised and ready for slaughter. Close the bathroom door, *agape mou*, and come over here so that I can take off your wedding dress as quickly as possible and make love to you, as I have been badly longing to do for so long.'

But Lucy felt paralysed and unable to move. Struck by unwanted fears and an apprehension which was making her limbs feel awkward and heavy. She was trying to blame it on the long day—on the tension leading up to the ceremony itself and the supreme weight of her heavy gown—but deep inside she knew the real cause of her anxiety.

She licked lips which had grown as dry as bone. Because she'd met Amy. She hadn't wanted to, but she'd liked Amy. She'd liked her very much. Her warm American voice had sounded both friendly and genuine. She'd found herself wishing that Amy had chosen her wedding dress because she was a damned sight sure it would have been more flattering than the one she'd ended up wearing. Remembering Milo's words, Lucy had even found herself wondering why Drakon hadn't married the stunning partner who'd been with him for years—when she seemed so beautiful and confident and fitted into his world much better than Lucy ever could.

Her confidence had been battered by the meeting but somehow she had managed to survive the toasts and the dancing before Drakon had whispered that it was time for them to slip away. And now she was standing nervously in the honeymoon suite of the Granchester Hotel, about to begin her married life with a man she didn't really know.

She swallowed, removing the fragrant garland of roses and the attached veil from her head and placing both on a nearby table. Should she ask if he still wanted to go through with this? If seeing Amy had made him realise what a dumb thing he'd done by marrying someone like Lucy Phillips? Because if he *had* changed his mind then perhaps they could still get the marriage annulled before they actually consummated it. She was certain that was legally possible and it would certainly be a mature thing to suggest. She opened her mouth to speak, but no words came. All she could feel was the rush of hot colour to her cheeks.

'Still she stands there like a frightened lamb, which makes me realise I shall have to come to you instead, my blushing bride.' Drakon's words were cajoling as he began to walk across the marbled floor towards her, but he moved with the stealthy intent of a dark panther who had just spotted its helpless prey. He had removed his jacket and tie and undone the top buttons of his dress shirt and, with his olive skin glowing and black hair ruffled, he looked relaxed and supremely poised. Unlike her, who was feeling completely overdressed and had started trembling violently, despite the warmth of the room.

He reached her at last and touched his fingertips to her cheek, slowly trailing their tips downwards until they reached the quivering outline of her lips. He bent to brush his mouth over hers in a slow kiss, before raising his head to look at her, his eyes still narrowed speculatively. 'Don't look so scared, Lucy,' he murmured. 'There's no reason to be. I mean, it isn't as if we've never done this before, is it?'

But never as man and wife, thought Lucy desperately—the sweet magic of his kiss fading as the enormity of her actions hit her. People said getting married needn't change anything but of course it did—otherwise, why would anyone bother? Because she wasn't just starry-eyed Lucy Phillips any more—the virgin who'd had a crush on him since for ever. Now she was the billionaire's wife and mother to his son—and suddenly she felt like an imposter. 'It just feels...different.'

'Then maybe we should stop overthinking it and just rely on our senses to do the work for us. What do you think? Turn around,' he said softly, without waiting for an answer.

She'd actually thought he couldn't bear to look at her anxious face but realised he wanted to undo each tiny hook of her wedding gown, his fingertips tiptoeing enticingly over her sensitive flesh. As the corseted bodice came apart and the cool air hit her skin, Lucy closed her eyes and silently practised different ways of asking the questions which had been plaguing her throughout the reception.

Tell me about Amy. How long have you known her? Have you ever made love to her? Or wanted to?

But Drakon's lips were following in the wake of his fingers. They were whispering over her back and trailing over her quivering flesh as he formed a featherlight path of kisses from neck to waist. Her skin flowered into goosepimples wherever he touched her and against her lacy bra, she could feel the insistent pushing of her nipples. Lucy sucked in a shuddering breath as he turned her around to face him again. The gleam of desire in his black eyes made something clench deep inside her and she wondered if she had taken complete leave of her senses. How could she possibly shatter the mood by asking him about another woman at a time like this?

'Now,' he murmured. 'Why don't we get rid of this dress completely?'

She heard the rueful note in his voice and was instantly on the defensive. 'You don't like it?'

He smiled as he traced a slow finger along the modest neckline of her very traditional gown. 'I thought it was perfectly appropriate for the entrance of my beautiful bride, but looser and freer is what I have in mind for what happens next.'

He slid the embossed satin of her gown over each shoulder and let the entire confection fall to the ground before effortlessly lifting her from the vast canopy of stiffened petticoats, until she was standing before him in just her white lacy underwear, hold-up stockings and spiky white high-heeled shoes. Slowly, he studied her and his black gaze felt as if it were scorching her skin where it lingered. 'Much better,' he said, and his voice was unsteady. 'Though I'm now feeling a little overdressed. Any ideas how we might redress the balance, Lucy?'

Lucy felt suddenly stricken with shyness as she lifted her fingers to his chest. Was he wondering what had happened to the uninhibited person she'd been back in the summer when he had awoken her sexuality and her appetite for him had been wild and untamed? She was wondering the same thing herself. But back then it had felt as if she had nothing to lose, while now the stakes seemed significantly higher. Yet wasn't she in danger of sabotaging their union before it had even started if she wasn't careful?

So snap out of it. Enjoy your wedding night

with your gorgeous new husband. Make this so good he'll never want to look elsewhere for his pleasure.

'I have some idea,' she murmured. 'Let me help you out of this shirt.'

She was so nervous she could barely undo the first button, but as soon as she made contact with his skin all her reservations melted away like honey left out in the midday sun. How could she have forgotten just how beautiful he was? His olive skin gleamed with health and vitality and hungrily she ran her gaze over all that hard, honed muscle. Her fingers drifted over his hair-roughened chest and Lucy heard him expel a shuddered sigh as she slipped the shirt from his shoulders and it slid to the ground. Which just left his trousers. She swallowed. It was easy to see how huge and taut his erection was, straining against the fine material, and her cheeks grew hot as she dropped her head to his shoulder.

'Oh,' she whispered against his neck, shy once more.

'Anyone would think you'd never seen me in such an intimate state before.'

She swallowed. 'It seems like a long time ago.'

'It seems like that to me, too,' he agreed

raggedly as he tugged at the belt of his trousers and swiftly bent to remove the rest of his clothes, his black eyes opaque with lust as he straightened up again. 'I've never had to wait for a woman like I've waited for you, Lucy. And it has been an exquisite kind of torture, do you realise that?'

Was it the thrill of the unknown which was making his voice dip with such husky intent as he unclipped her bra, so that her breasts sprang free against his bare chest? Did novelty alone account for the tense shudder which ran through his big body as he tugged her panties down over her thighs and kicked them impatiently away, before dextrously disposing of her high heels and filmy stockings so that they ended up in a white heap on the floor? Lucy didn't know and, right then, she didn't particularly care because he was lifting her into his arms and carrying her over to the bed, laying her down in the centre of the vast mattress like a willing sacrifice. His gaze moved down over her body. He stroked his fingers over her breasts, her belly, her hips, his narrowing eyes noting the restless wriggle of her bare bottom against the duvet. And then he smiled.

'Want me?' he questioned softly.

'You know I do,' she whispered.

He lay down on top of her, pushing her hair back from her flushed face before bending his head to kiss her. And as Lucy opened her eager lips to meet his, she felt a powerful wave of emotion rushing through her. Because *this* was the bit she remembered best. The sensation of his flesh pressing against hers. The long, drugging kisses and entwining of limbs and the feeling that this was somehow *meant* to be. Eagerly, she touched him back, and he moaned softly as she stroked him, and for a while they both seemed content with a rapt and silent rediscovery of each other's bodies. And then suddenly the tempo seemed to change. Drakon's body became taut as he captured her arms above her head and held them against the pillow, before pressing his mouth to her nipple so that she could feel the warmth of his breath against the erect skin.

'Oh,' she gasped softly.

'I love your breasts, Lucy,' he said huskily. 'They're so damned…big.'

As if to illustrate his pleasure, he began licking what felt like every inch of her, making her squirm with helpless delight. And meantime his hand had slipped between her legs and was spreading open her thighs, one finger thrumming urgently against her creamy heat so that Lucy's head fell back against the pillow. His rhythm was blissful and relentless—it rocketed her straight up to the stars and she came very quickly, her body arching beneath his hand as the spasms clenched low in her belly and then reverberated through her body like a sweet, spent storm. And when at last her eyelids fluttered open, it was to meet the black gleam of his penetrating gaze.

'And I like watching you come,' he observed throatily. 'I like it when your body goes rigid and you make those gasping little sounds at the back of your throat.'

These were starkly sensual statements which only an hour ago might have had her blushing like a schoolgirl, but not now—not when satisfaction was flooding through her still-pulsing body. Yet despite the intense pleasure which had transformed her, it wasn't enough, Lucy decided. Not nearly enough. Because she was no longer just some random woman he'd ended up having unexpected sex with on his private Greek island. She was now his wife and she wanted him to make love to her properly. She wanted him inside her. Badly. Reaching her arms up around his neck, she pulled his head down, and as his lips met hers a restless heat begin to rise inside her once more. She heard him give a low laugh as his tongue slipped inside her mouth and he began to circle his hips in a provocative demonstration of his arousal, until she thought she would go crazy with longing.

She realised he was rolling away from her and, for one illogical moment, wondered if her earlier fears had materialised and he was actually having second thoughts about consummating the marriage. But his reasoning was far more pragmatic than that. He was reaching for something on the bedside locker and Lucy swallowed when she saw what it was. A condom. Of *course* he would wear a condom. She could feel faint hysteria—and fear—spiral up inside her, because he'd told her he didn't want any more children and he was just making sure that wouldn't happen. He wasn't to know that protection was completely unnecessary in her case, was he?

'Drakon?'

His eyes were smoky with lust as he turned round. *'Ti?'*

'I'm… I'm on the pill.'

He smiled approvingly as he dropped the condom back on the nightstand. 'What excellent planning, my clever wife,' he murmured. 'That's exactly as it should be.'

Hysteria began to build again. Should she tell him she'd been on the pill for years because of her endometriosis? But by then he was rolling back towards her, pulling her into his arms with a groan of feral hunger, and Lucy could feel his naked hardness touching against her moist heat. He bent his dark head and was kissing her with a thoroughness which was making her heart want to burst out of her chest, because when he kissed her like that it felt like a fairy tale. And why would she risk destroying that by talking about her tragic gynaecological history at a time like this, when none of it related to their marriage plans?

'Now,' he breathed as he eased himself inside her. '*Evge!* You are so tight, Lucy. So very tight, my sweet little virgin.'

'But I'm not…' She gasped as he began to drive up deep inside her. 'I'm not a virgin any more.'

'Always,' he contradicted as his body took on an exquisite rhythm. 'Always to me.'

Did his raw words intensify her pleasure? Possibly. Again, Lucy came very quickly and so did he—and all her fears about the amazing chemistry they shared being some sort of fluke were banished. Afterwards she lay sleepy and sated in his arms but she felt him stir almost immediately and they did it all over again. And again. They did it so many times that she lost count and she must have dozed off, because the next thing she knew she was being woken by the sound of Big Ben chiming out midnight. But as the last chime faded into the night, Lucy knew she had to ask him the question which was still gnawing away at her—because otherwise wouldn't she just keep torturing herself with fevered imaginings?

She waited until he had poured two glasses of champagne and brought them back to bed, but her own drink lay untouched on the nightstand as she glanced over at Drakon's autocratic profile. He had picked up his phone and was reading something off the screen and Lucy cleared her throat, trying to make her words sound as nonchalant as possible. 'You seem very close to Amy,' she observed.

'Mmm…' he said absently as he put the phone back on the locker, screen side down. 'We've known each other a long time.'

Make it casual. All you're doing is find-

ing out a bit more about him and the people in his life.

She tried to keep her voice bright but her words sounded as forced as the last bit of toothpaste you tried to squeeze from the tube. 'So how did you first get into partnership with her?'

There was a pause as he turned to look at her, his black gaze mocking. 'You really want to talk about this right now?'

Of course she didn't. She wanted him to put his glass down and pull her into his arms and tell her he was starting to fall in love with her, but that was never going to happen, not in a million years. And in the meantime she had to face down her nameless fears or allow them to grow. To grow and run the risk of dominating her thoughts and ruining her relationship, even if it was a relationship which fell short of her dreams. 'I'm just interested,' she said blandly. 'And as your wife, it's useful if I find out as much as I can about you. There's loads about your past which is a mystery to me.'

Drakon took a sip of champagne and leaned back against the bank of feathered pillows. He didn't particularly feel like talking—but the sex had been so damned hot that he was feeling unusually accommodating towards his new bride. 'Me and Amy,' he mused. 'I guess it was one of those lucky meetings.'

'Sort of...star-crossed?' she ventured casually.

He shrugged, wondering why women always complicated things—or was she just trying to impress him with overblown quotes from Shakespeare? 'I don't know about that,' he said, a little impatiently. 'We were both working at the same office in Hong Kong and one night I decided to ask her out for dinner.'

'Because you fancied her?'

Drakon frowned. She might have been a virgin until very recently, but surely she wasn't *that* naïve? Because Lucy was practical. A practical and realistic woman who'd experienced her own share of bad stuff. Surely one thing which could come out of this unplanned marriage was the ability to be completely honest with her, because wasn't honesty the quality he valued above all else?

'Who wouldn't fancy her?' he questioned, barely registering the way she flinched, because by then his jaw had tightened with the memory of those turbulent days. 'I was in a bad place,' he admitted. 'My father's will had just been read to reveal that he'd basically blown the entire Konstantinou fortune during his lifetime. And my brother had gone ballistic when he'd discovered there was nothing left for him to inherit.'

'And you must have been disappointed to discover that you'd lost your own expected share of the family fortune?' she suggested.

He shook his head. 'That would never have been the case. The laws of primogeniture meant that, as the eldest son, Niko would have inherited everything.'

'And you never minded that?'

'Of course I minded! I'm not some sort of saint, Lucy.' His mouth twisted into a hard smile. 'But I'd resigned myself to my fate a long time earlier. And underneath it all, I discovered I was less like my father and more like my grandfather, who had worked his way up from the bottom to the very top. I knew I could make my own way in the world and that's exactly what I was doing. I'd been to university and got myself a decent degree and was a petrochemical engineer, working for a big company in the Far East.'

'But employees of big companies don't tend to make billions of dollars,' observed Lucy slowly. 'They don't own private jets or private islands or spend hundreds of thousands of pounds on last-minute weddings in luxury hotels.'

'No, they don't. And that's where Amy came in.' Drakon's voice became thoughtful. 'She was a geologist—the best geologist I've ever come across. After she'd explained she wasn't interested in me romantically, she told me that she'd seen the potential for oil on one of the Indonesian islands, but didn't have the wherewithal to explore it. And that's where *I* came in.' He paused. 'I believed in her passion and enthusiasm and my gut feeling told me she was onto something big. I'd just received a huge bonus from the company but I was growing bored and frustrated with working for someone else. I told Amy I was prepared to back her hunch but that we needed to really go for it. So we chartered a small company to do the drilling for us, and within six months we'd struck oil.' He took another sip of champagne and sighed. 'Best feeling in the world,' he reflected.

'I'm sure it was,' she said woodenly.

He turned to look at her. The rosy flush which had made her skin glow after a rapid succession of orgasms might never have happened, for her face was as pale as it had been just before she'd taken her wedding vows. He felt a flicker of irritation, because surely ir-rational mood swings had no place in what they had both agreed was to be a purely func-tional marriage. 'Is something wrong?' he questioned coolly.

Lucy wanted to jump up from the bed and rail at him for his insensitivity. To tell him that yes, of *course* there was something wrong. It was the first night of their honey-moon and not only had he confided that dis-covering oil was better than having sex with his new bride—he'd also confessed that the gorgeous Amy had once turned him down!

But one thing puzzled her more than her very natural feminine outrage at his reac-tion. Because Drakon was a determined and charismatic man who attracted women like ants to honey. Who was to say that Amy mightn't have lived to regret her impetuos-ity in refusing a relationship with someone like him—especially once he had decided to adopt Xander?

'So when Xander was orphaned, you weren't at all tempted to ask Amy to marry you, just in case she'd changed her mind?' she questioned slowly. 'Seeing as how you know each other so well and clearly get on.'

He narrowed his eyes and seemed to be

running something over in his mind because it took a moment or two before he answered. 'That was never going to be on the cards, because I needed not just a mother, but a wife in the fullest sense of the word.' There was another pause. 'Amy's gay, Lucy,' he said eventually. 'She explained that at the time. She just hadn't come out to her family about it yet. She still hasn't. Like I said, you were my first choice. My only choice, really.'

Lucy supposed he must be paying her a compliment but somehow it didn't feel like one. Somehow it felt like being second-best and that wasn't such a great way to start married life. She turned to pick up her champagne glass but the fizzing bubbles only seemed to emphasise the flatness of her mood, when she realised that Drakon was sitting up in bed and pointing out of the enormous picture windows opposite.

'Will you take a look at that?' he exclaimed softly, his Greek accent velvety and pronounced.

She turned to follow the direction of his gaze, where the dazzle of the city was just visible through the bare branches of the trees—but that wasn't what had caught the tycoon's attention. It was the giant snowflakes which were tumbling from the sky like acrobats, turning golden in the bright light which streamed from the hotel windows.

'It's snowing,' said Lucy dutifully, trying to replicate his wonder since she supposed it was rare to see snow in Greece. But the irony of this final fairy-tale aspect to her Christmas wedding didn't escape her.

She was lying in a rumpled bed, having had mind-blowing sex with her stunning bridegroom, while outside the world was magically turning white. It was like something out of a movie.

But just like a movie—none of it was real.

CHAPTER SEVEN

THE PRESS WERE out in force next morning when the newly-weds left the Granchester Hotel in a flurry of flashbulbs. Drakon's hand was pressed lightly against Lucy's back as he guided her through the scrum of photographers and she looked up at him in gratitude just as the flash went off. And that was the photo which made the online edition of Britain's biggest tabloid. Lucy Konstantinou, standing by the giant hotel Christmas tree with shining eyes and snowflakes on her nose, while Drakon looked down at her with something indeterminate written on his hard and handsome face.

On the way to the airfield Lucy insisted on stopping by the apartment to check on Xander, but the baby was fast asleep and Sofia was assembling a new interactive baby mat with bells and squeaky cushions, for when he awoke. The nanny had looked up when they'd walked in, a question creasing her eyes, as if surprised to see them. Almost as if this un-scheduled stop was as unwelcome to her as it had been to Drakon.

'Satisfied?' her new husband had de-manded as the limousine had pulled away from the kerb and Lucy had nodded before staring out of the window at the falling snow, feeling kind of *extraneous*. Not a real wife, nor a real mother either, it seemed.

There were photos of them boarding the plane at Northolt, where the fields surround-ing the airstrip were soft and white and more clouds of snowflakes swirled from the sky. There was even a shot from inside the wed-ding reception—though it was a mystery who had taken it—in which she and Drakon had been feeding each other hunks of creamy wedding cake.

Nobody would have guessed from that laughing image that at that precise moment Lucy had been in an agony of self-doubt about Amy and her place in Drakon's life. Yet now that fear had been banished and they were just about to begin their married life to-gether and everything should be just fine and dandy, shouldn't it?

Shouldn't it?

Cosseted in the luxury of Drakon's plane, Lucy scrolled down the newspaper website past all the pictures. *English Nurse Marries Greek Billionaire!* ran the headline, and she found herself wondering why newspapers seemed obsessed with stereotypes.

Her smile was wry. Or maybe they were simply more perceptive than she gave them credit for. Perhaps they had homed into her dreamlike state before, during and after the ceremony—and managed to work out for themselves that this all felt as if it were happening to someone else, not her.

The jet flew them straight to Prasinisos and once Drakon had dismissed the flight attendants, he pulled her into his arms and started to kiss her. And wasn't it strange how sex could melt away your misgivings? Because the only thing she seemed able to rely on was her body's reaction whenever Drakon touched her. It had only been a few hours since they'd last made love but already she was hungry to feel him inside her again. To feel him and taste him and shudder out her pleasure as he filled her with his thrusting hardness. Inside the plane's master bedroom, he peeled off her clothes with care, as if he were slowly unwrapping a Christmas present, and he laughed when she tugged at his clothes with more eagerness than finesse.

'Are you going to rip my shirt off, Lucy?'

'If you could be bothered to help me with the buttons that wouldn't be an option.'

'Or maybe I'm enjoying being the passive object of your desire?'

'You? Passive? I don't think so.'

'I don't think so either,' he growled, pushing her back on the bed to bury his dark head beneath her thighs, so that she had to bite at the knuckles of one hand to prevent herself from shouting out her pleasure. Eventually he moved back up her body and thrust deep inside her and she could feel the shimmering of another intense orgasm waiting in the wings. Afterwards she repaired her hair as best she could but her cheeks still had a fiery glow as the plane touched down on his private island.

It felt strange to be back. Last time Lucy had visited Prasinisos had been for an unexpected freebie weekend when it had been impossible not to be overawed by the beauty of Drakon's exclusive home. But she'd also been aware of how broke she was in comparison to her wealthy host—a difference which had been brought home when his driver had been sent to meet her, widening his eyes before quickly composing himself.

That same driver was here today—Stavros, his name was—but there was no such look of bewilderment on his face. Maybe he didn't even recognise her as the same woman. Why, when she'd looked into the mirror this morning Lucy had barely recognised herself! Her designer clothes were exquisitely cut and hugely flattering and she knew that the cost of her shoes and handbag had been eye-wateringly high. She *looked* expensive and felt expensive—as if she had every right to be married to one of the world's wealthiest men. But inside she was the same Lucy, wasn't she? The woman who was not really a complete woman, married to a man who seemed indifferent to love and emotion.

But unless she wanted to ruin this honeymoon, she was going to have to put a lid on her insecurities. To learn how to manage and adjust them. She had just married the most amazing man and was about to experience the holiday of a lifetime and she owed it to them both to make the very best of it.

Drakon was quiet as they drove up the rugged path towards his cliff-top villa past the dramatic outcrop of rock which some people said resembled a man's face. He could feel the tension of the last few weeks leeching from his body, and not simply because of the post-sex endorphins which were lingering after that amazing mid-flight encounter with his new wife. No. It was a sense of achievement which now prevailed because it had all worked out exactly as he'd planned. He'd pulled it off. He had gained a suitable mother for his baby nephew and all he needed to do now was to play the part of contented newly-wed with conviction. Still, if the first twenty-four hours of married life were anything to go by, that shouldn't be too difficult. Leaning back against the leather seat, he gave a small smile as Lucy's excited voice broke into his reflection.

'Look! Over there. What's that, Drakon?'

He narrowed his eyes in the direction of her pointing finger. 'It's a peregrine falcon. Never seen one before?'

'I'm not sure. And if I did I wouldn't know what to call it.'

'Call yourself a country girl?' he teased.

'As you know, I only live an hour outside London, which is hardly rural isolation,' she protested as she leaned forward to get a better look at the falcon. 'Wow. That's amazing. So fast and so graceful.'

'And so deadly,' he commented, deadpan. 'To small mammals, at any rate.'

'I suppose so.' She turned to look at him. 'And the sea is very blue. Do you suppose there's any chance of going swimming?'

Drakon thought how wistful her voice sounded and was reminded of the first time he'd seen her here—with her body ploughing through the azure waters of his pool. 'It's December, Lucy,' he reminded her gently.

'And people in the UK swim in all weathers,' she informed him. 'In the newspapers recently was a photo of a woman in Scotland who had to smash her way through the ice with a pickaxe before she could go for her daily swim.'

He laughed. 'I'm not sure I'd trust you with a pickaxe. We'll see. But not today. Today I have only one thing in mind and that's to take my beautiful wife to bed as quickly as possible.'

Lucy wanted to object. To tell him not to say things like that because she wasn't beautiful and they sounded dangerously romantic and she was afraid of getting sucked into a vortex of false promise, which would make her long for things which were never going to happen. Because flattering words didn't really mean anything, did they? They were just words.

They reached the palatial villa where all the staff were lined up to greet them and it was only after she had shaken everyone's hands that Lucy noticed the giant decorated tree which was glittering in one corner of the vast sitting room which led off the marbled foyer.

'I didn't know you had Christmas trees in Greece,' she said wonderingly as she gazed at lush branches strewn with stars and fairy lights.

'On the contrary, we love them. Sub-zero temperatures aren't obligatory,' answered Drakon with soft mockery in his voice. 'On Christmas Eve the children sing carols and carry model boats painted gold and decorated with nuts. And we give presents, of course.'

Lucy thought about the modest gift she had tucked away for him in her suitcase and realised how humble it would appear in this lavish setting, as Drakon led her upstairs to the vast bedroom which overlooked the Mediterranean. The room was full of bright light and winter sunshine but she found herself glancing around nervously, and her voice was diffident when she spoke. 'It looks...*different* in here.'

'It is.' The sweeping movement of his hand indicated the pristine linen adorning the king-size bed, as well as a soft new shade of grey on the walls. 'I decided to have the room redecorated before you got here.'

She was silent for a moment. 'Oh? And why was that?'

'Does it matter why?'

Lucy tried to stem the question but she couldn't. Afterwards she would try to justify it by reasoning that she needed to know exactly where she stood, but perhaps it was more like worrying a healing cut on your finger and inadvertently making it bleed again. 'I think so,' she said lightly. 'Aren't we supposed to be honest with each other now we're married?'

There was a pause. 'I just thought it would be good to start afresh, with a completely clean slate.'

'You mean, we'll be using sheets which haven't been slept in by any other woman?'

He winced. 'If you like.'

She nodded, hating the completely unreasonable urge to cry which was making her eyes prickle. She knew the reality because he'd painstakingly spelt it out for her in London, just so there could be no mistake. He'd explained that he hadn't been sexually indiscriminate but, even so, of *course* he'd had plenty of lovers before her. And why *shouldn't* he? *She* was the freak, not Drakon. She was the woman approaching thirty who'd never been intimate with anyone until she'd melted into the arms of her Greek lover.

'But won't you miss it, Drakon?' she forced herself to question huskily. 'The variety of having all those different lovers? Though maybe I'm being presumptuous in assuming there won't be any in the future. We've never discussed whether this is going to be an open marriage before now, have we?'

Drakon could hear the bravado in her voice and admired her outspokenness, knowing that few women would have been so matter-of-fact about such a tricky subject. Until he reminded himself that her candour was only possible because neither of them had any real emotion invested in the relationship. And that was why this marriage had a chance of succeeding—*because* there were no unrealistic expectations of love. And if she wanted honesty, didn't he owe her that? His mouth hardened. Of course he did. Especially when he found lies so detestable.

'I thought I'd made it clear that I would pledge to you my sexual loyalty,' he said coolly. 'Because I know how destructive infidelity can be. I'm not planning on having anyone other than you as my lover, Lucy, because sexually you thrill me in every way.' He sucked in a deep breath. 'But right now I'm having difficulty talking because the desire to pin you down on that bed and lose myself deep inside your body is pushing everything else from my mind.'

'Then what are you waiting for?' she questioned shakily.

He could hear the relief in her voice as he walked towards her, enjoying the instinctive darkening of her eyes as he unbuttoned her coat and hung it over the back of a chair. 'You seem to be wearing rather a lot of clothes,' he complained as he bent to unzip her knee-high boots.

'It was s-snowing when we left the Granchester, if you remember,' she breathed, perching on the edge of the bed as he slid the soft leather over each calf.

'Well, it isn't snowing here.'

She lifted her hips accommodatingly to

allow him to slither her skirt over them. 'Does it ever snow on the island?' she queried conversationally.

'I didn't bring you here to discuss the damned weather,' he growled. 'We're not in England now.'

He undressed her efficiently and though on some level he registered the fine fabric and cut of her new clothes, it was the naked Lucy which made his senses soar like the peregrine falcon which had swooped through the sky on the journey here. His fingers skated over her big, pale breasts and traced featherlight paths over her arching ribcage and although he was rock-hard and eager to thrust deep inside her, he made himself wait. As he slowly kissed her belly and licked a teasing line downwards, he lifted his head to look at her.

'You've waxed,' he observed, one demonstrative finger circling the satin-smooth skin of her inner thigh. 'I noticed it last night but was a little too...*preoccupied* to mention it.'

'Drakon!'

'You want to be intimate in all ways?' he mused. 'Or do you want always to behave like a virgin and talk like a virgin?'

She shook her head. 'The...the wedding dress designer advised I get it done.' She gasped as his finger dipped lower. 'She said she thought…less is more—'

'Except concerning the application of sequins, of course,' he commented drily as he moved over her.

He made it last as long as he could—which was precisely long enough to allow them both to choke out their almost simultaneous pleasure. The second time he took it more slowly, enjoying Lucy's cries of wonder as her nails dug into his shoulder. When eventually they fell asleep, the setting sun was blazing through the huge windows so that the interior of the bedroom resembled a coral furnace. And when they woke, diamond-bright stars had been dusted over the clear, night sky. Drakon clicked on a lamp to see Lucy struggling to open her eyes, her nut-brown hair spread like satin over the pillow.

'What time is it?' she enquired sleepily.

'Dinner time.' He glanced over at his wristwatch. 'At least, it will be soon. Spiro was in the process of preparing a wedding feast and if you want to shower—'

'I do. I won't take long.'

'Take as long as you like. This room has two bathrooms.'

She nodded and rose from the bed but she

didn't lean over and kiss him and, for Drakon, it felt as if all the intimacies of the previous few hours hadn't happened. As if she'd filed them all away under Sexy Lucy and gone back to being Sensible Lucy. He told himself he liked it that way. That it would be easier if they compartmentalised their lives like that all the time. But then she went and spoilt it all.

'Drakon?'

Something in the way she said his name warned him, for it contained that curious note of emphasis which women made whenever they were about to start prying. Perhaps hoping to distract her with the sight of his ever-present desire, he pushed back the rumpled duvet and got out of bed. 'What?'

But she deliberately kept her gaze fixed on his face, not his groin. 'Earlier on, when you said…when you said you knew how destructive infidelity can be… Were you talking about your own experiences?'

He made no attempt to hide his displeasure. 'Does it really matter?'

'I think it does, yes. Did someone cheat on you?'

In a way, yes, though not in the way he

suspected she meant. 'Go and have your shower, Lucy.'

'But—'

'I said *go*.'

He went into the second bathroom and stood beneath the fierce jets of the shower before quickly shaving and dressing and hoping Lucy would have had the sense to forget it and move on. But when eventually she'd finished getting ready—standing in front of him in a velvet dress the colour of the night sky outside the window—he could see that look of stubborn determination still on her face.

'Are we going to talk about it?' she questioned.

'About what?' he said, deliberately misunderstanding.

'About the infidelity you were referring to earlier.'

'It's nothing.'

'Doesn't sound like nothing to me. And weren't you the one who suggested the necessity of intimacy in this relationship?'

It was a clever twisting of his own words and Drakon felt trapped—but he could hardly storm out of the room and tell her to go to hell, could he? Not on the second night of his honeymoon. 'Is this what they taught you to do at nursing school, Lucy?' he demanded. 'To keep digging and digging until you got your answer?'

Biting back an exclamation of impatience, he walked over to the dressing table and extracted a pair of golden cufflinks from one of the drawers. But he was aware that he was playing for time and he suspected Lucy was aware of it, too. He could sense her watching him, and waiting—but the overriding feeling he was getting from her was one of compassion rather than prurience. And suddenly Drakon found himself wondering why he was so intent on keeping his memories locked away, because it wasn't as if anything he told her was going to affect the practical nature of their relationship, was it?

Slowly, he slotted the second cufflink in place so that it lay flush and gleaming against the cream silk. Mightn't it be a relief to confide in her something he'd only ever discussed with his mother? His mouth twisted. His lying mother. He felt the knot of pain in his gut tighten as he turned back to face his new wife.

'Okay.' He watched as she sat down on the end of the bed, her eyes fixed unwaveringly on his face, and it was only then that he began to speak. 'You're probably aware that I grew up in extreme luxury?'

She gave a short laugh. 'There were no poor boys at Milton school, Drakon.'

He nodded. 'No. I guess there weren't,' he agreed thoughtfully. 'My father was the only child of an extremely wealthy man, but he didn't follow my grandfather into the business. In fact, he'd never worked—he just lived off the profits of the company which my grandfather had painstakingly built up from scratch. Maybe the fact that everything had always been handed to him on a plate and the lack of purpose in his life were what lay behind what I was to later discover were his fundamental lack of self-worth and low self-esteem. But from the outside, at least, things looked perfect. He married my mother, who worshipped the ground he walked on, which only made his sense of entitlement all the greater. Everything she did was for my father. It was my first experience of unconditional female adoration, though it certainly wasn't to be my last. She spent the majority of her time completely preoccupied with her appearance. Trying to stay young. Trying to fight nature's natural progression with one surgical procedure after another. By the time she was in her forties, her face was so cosmetically altered that she could barely move her mouth to smile.'

'And what was she like towards you—and Niko?'

'We were superfluous to requirements. In short, we got in the way.' His mouth twisted. 'When Niko and I were seven they sent us away to school in England, and after that I felt as though I had two very different lives. My life in England and my life in Greece. But every time I went home on vacation, I could sense things weren't right. I remember the atmosphere as being incredibly *tense*. I knew the marriage wasn't happy, but since I had no idea what a happy marriage looked like, I just accepted it. But things seemed to be getting worse and every time I asked my mother if anything was wrong she would just fob me off and tell me everything was just fine. Tell me that my father was nothing less than a genius and it was none of my business.'

'But it wasn't fine?' she interjected, into the silence which followed.

He gave a bitter laugh. 'You could say that. Behind the scenes everything was breaking down at an unbelievable speed. She knew that and she must have known how the outcome of the decline would impact on all our lives but she lied to me.' His voice grew silent for a moment. 'But it wasn't until my father's death that it came out just how comprehensively she'd lied. One sordid fact came spilling out after another—and the bubble which had been the perceived perfection of Konstantinou family life burst in the most spectacular way.'

'How?'

He didn't answer straight away and when he did, he winced, as if he had just bitten into something sour. 'I learned that for years my father had been entertaining a series of high-class hookers. Women who indulged him in whatever depravity was his current favourite and, from what I could gather, there were plenty of those. In turn he indulged them with whatever took their fancy—anything ranging from large diamonds to fancy apartments. He became a regular at the world's biggest casinos and high-rollers like him always attract a following of low-lifers. As a result, the business was in tatters and there was barely anything left. It wasn't what Niko had been led to believe would be his inheritance and that was the beginning of his descent into addiction. That was when he disappeared. I should have done something,' he added bitterly. 'I should have prevented it.'

'But what could you have done, Drakon?' she questioned urgently. 'Because I'm getting the feeling that you're shouldering most of the blame here.'

Drakon clenched his fists as familiar feelings of anger and frustration pulsed through him. 'Because by then I had some idea how commerce worked and could have helped,' he bit out. 'I could have found some sort of rescue package to have halted the decline of the company, or implored my father to seek help. If my mother had told me the truth instead of pretending nothing was wrong, then I could have done everything in my power to turn it around.'

She shook her head. 'But sometimes the best will in the world won't make people do what you want them to do!' she said, holding the palms of her hands towards him in silent appeal. 'Even if you'd known about it, your father might have blocked all your attempts to save the company—he might still have chosen his life of depravity. Sometimes you're powerless to do anything except sit back and watch while other people make their own mistakes, and there's absolutely nothing you can do about it.'

But Drakon shook his head, closing his heart and his ears to what she was saying. 'I don't do powerless, Lucy,' he said. 'Not any more. That's something you need to know about me. Maybe the only thing.'

His words tailed away as the bells from the village church began ringing out and he could hear the sound of the children beginning to sing the traditional *kalandra*, but Drakon found himself unable to feel any sense of joyful celebration as he glanced down at his watch.

It was Christmas Day.

CHAPTER EIGHT

PUSHING ASIDE THE festive wrapping paper, Lucy felt her eyes widen as she pulled a circlet of glittering diamonds from the dark leather box. 'Oh, Drakon,' she said.

'Do you like it?'

'How could anyone not like it?' she questioned shakily, slipping the bracelet over her wrist and holding it up in the air so that it sparkled like a ring of rainbows in the winter sunshine. But the truth was that it felt too expensive. Too impersonal—and nothing like the ink-spot sapphire which he'd picked out himself. She wanted to know who'd chosen it but she also didn't *want* to know, for fear that it might have been Amy or one of his assistants. And in the meantime—how humble was her own little present going to look in comparison to this?

A little awkwardly, she walked over to the

Christmas tree and bent to retrieve the gift she'd placed there earlier. 'It's not very much,' she said as she handed it to him.

'I'm sure it will be perfect,' said her new husband, his voice carrying the bland reassurance of someone who was impossible to buy for.

But she saw his face change as he pulled out a small picture from within the neat folds of holly-strewn paper.

'You don't like it?' she questioned anxiously as he stared at it in silence.

'I... It's a line drawing of Prasinisos,' he said slowly, lifting his head to look at her. 'Where on earth did you get it?'

'I found it in London just before the wedding. There's a tiny shop in an arcade close to Leicester Square station which specialises in maps and drawings of small islands. I couldn't believe it when I saw it there. You haven't already got it, have you?'

He shook his head as he turned it over, his thumb caressing the worn leather frame, and an odd kind of smile touched the corners of his lips. 'No, I haven't got it.'

'I know it's only—'

'It's not *only* anything,' he corrected, almost fiercely. 'It's probably the most personal gift anyone has ever bought me. And now I think I'd better thank you properly, don't you?'

Lucy smiled and bit her lip. 'If you like.'

'I really did think you might have learned to stop blushing by now.' He gave a low laugh and she felt as if she'd just won the lottery. 'Come here.'

It was a Yuletide like no other Lucy had ever experienced, but then she'd spent so many of them on her own these past few years that maybe she had simply forgotten what it was like to celebrate. For lunch they sat down to a festive feast which had been prepared for them by Spiros, the chef. There were shiny crackers and napkins embroidered with stars on the table, and shiny *christopsomo* bread, which was traditionally eaten on Christmas Day. The delicious loaf was flavoured with cinnamon, oranges and cloves and Drakon told her that it translated literally as 'Christ's bread'. Afterwards, they ate lamb with salad and a delicious walnut-covered cake called *melomakarono*—which was also traditional.

After retiring to their bedroom for a sex-jammed siesta, Drakon drove her to his favourite cove, a curving crescent of deepest blue, and Lucy kicked off her shoes immediately, feeling the pale, soft sand between her toes as she gazed out at the glimmering horizon. 'I'd love to go for a swim,' she said, a little wistfully.

'It's way too cold.'

'I guess.' She sighed. 'Anyway, it's pointless wishing because I haven't brought my costume.'

'And because only a crazy person would swim on a day like this.'

Lucy stared out at the sapphire water on which the winter sunshine was dancing in undulating lines of liquid gold, telling herself that this might be Greece but it was still winter and Drakon was probably right—only a crazy person would want to swim on Christmas Day. Yet something was compelling her to take to the water and she couldn't work out if it was just a sense of feeling so intensely alive, or the powerful sense of hope which had been building up inside her since their plane had touched down on Prasinisos. Because despite her initial misgivings about the trip, this felt as if it was rapidly turning into a proper honeymoon. Not just the sex, which had been perfect as always—but because Drakon had revealed a chink in his steely armour and allowed her to look inside at the man beneath. He had confided stuff about his family which made her understand him a little better and didn't that spell only positive things for their future together?

He was standing silhouetted against the shoreline, his black hair ruffled and the light breeze blowing at his linen shirt, which was tucked into a pair of faded jeans, and he looked so utterly gorgeous that a thrill of pleasure ran through her. Was that what made her feel so uninhibited? Why she suddenly peeled her sweater over her head and dropped it on the sand, before starting to unbutton her jeans?

His black eyes narrowed as the denim slid to the sand. 'Now what are you doing?'

'What does it look like?'

'You're not planning on going *skinny-dipping* are you, Lucy?'

She registered his tone of mocking incredulity and forced herself to focus on her smile rather than the goosebumps which greeted the removal of her jeans. 'Why not?' she queried innocently as she unclipped her bra and wriggled out of her knickers. 'Didn't you say you owned this beach and nobody ever came near it?'

She relished the look in his eyes as she

turned to pound across the beach and ran into the water. She was too intent on forcing herself to plunge straight beneath the icy depths to take any notice of what Drakon might be doing, but she was curving her arm into a powerful front crawl when she realised he was swimming right beside her, black hair plastered to his head like a seal, his naked body gleaming olive-gold underneath the water. In silent acknowledgement of his unspoken challenge, Lucy set off, racing in a line parallel to the shore, and gave it everything she had. She was the strongest female swimmer she knew, but it wasn't nearly enough to beat her powerhouse of a husband.

He made it look so effortless and was barely out of breath when eventually she swam into his waiting arms, and he laughed against her wet neck and kissed it over and over again as she wrapped her legs around his back. The exercise had given her immunity against the chilly sea and it felt perfectly natural for Drakon's hands to begin a sensual exploration of her body beneath the surface of the water. And perfectly natural for her to do the same to him. His mouth was on hers— it tasted salty and cold and her nipples were like bullets as they pressed into his chest. A small butterfly beat of awareness at her clitoris was making itself insistently known and he gave a small groan of pleasure when she curled her fingers around his hardness.

'I want to do it to you now,' he whispered.

'Then do it,' she whispered back.

He covered her mouth with his seeking lips and Lucy's brain just went to mush. His lips were on her neck and then her breasts. His hungry fingers were parting her aching folds and as he nudged his moist tip against her, she tightened the grip of her legs around the jut of his hips. She gasped with pleasure as he made that first thrust, tilting to accommodate the huge width of him, and the angle of his penetration made her gasp some more. She came very quickly, glad he was supporting her buttocks as he choked out his own fulfilment, and she could feel the rough rasp of his jaw as his head sank against her shoulder, his mouth pressing against her wet hair.

'I never thought I'd make love in the sea,' she said, once she could trust herself to speak again.

'And your verdict?'

'It was…*okay*,' she said, and he laughed.

'Just okay?'

She shrugged.

'Then maybe I'd better do it to you again,' he growled with soft intent and Lucy only pretended to run away from him.

Afterwards they swam back to shore and dressed with numb fingers, hastily pulling clothes onto their still-damp bodies. But any coldness was forgotten the moment they got back to the heated car where soft blankets were stashed on the back seat and Drakon must have arranged for Spiros to make a thermos of creamy hot chocolate, lightly laced with brandy, which they drank from a shared cup.

'Drakon?'

'Mmm?'

'Did you…did you *plan* this?' questioned Lucy suspiciously, surveying him across a cloud of steam.

'The outing?'

'The sex.'

There was a pause. 'Put it this way, I like to cover every eventuality.' The smile he gave her was automatic but suddenly Drakon found himself looking away from her searching blue gaze to stare at the horizon ahead. He swallowed, still reeling from the intensity of what had happened back there in the water. Not just because it had been outside—he certainly wasn't a secret exhibitionist craving to be observed *in flagrante*—and he'd meant what he said when he'd told Lucy that his beach was completely private.

No. It wasn't that. It had more to do with the closeness he'd felt when their bodies had been locked together in that urgent, underwater coupling. Almost as if they'd been part of the same body. It had felt…*unsettling*. Disturbing. It had brought with it echoes of the past. Of things happening which were outside his control—and that was a feeling he'd vowed never to replicate. More than that— hadn't he felt the twist of something unknown in his heart when she'd held her face up to his and he'd started to kiss her? There was something about her sweet enthusiasm which was difficult to resist and that wasn't the only thing about her which was dangerous. Somehow she'd manged to peel away some of the defensive layers which were such an intrinsic part of his make-up. He'd talked about stuff he usually kept locked away and in the process she'd made him feel as if she'd burrowed inside his head.

He felt his skin icing as he started up the engine and the four-by-four ascended the cliff road, past the rocky outline of the man's face.

Well, it wasn't going to happen again. She wasn't going to get any closer than she already had and maybe he needed to show her that, once this honeymoon was over. Despite the thoughtfulness of her Christmas present, which had affected him in a way he hadn't been expecting, it didn't actually *mean* anything, did it? This was never intended to be anything more than a marriage of convenience and it was pretty *inconvenient* to have a wife who was always prying like that. He was silent on the drive back to the villa and glad when his phone started vibrating the moment they entered the complex and he could excuse himself to deal with a phone call from one of his brokers in New York.

'I'm not sure how long this will take,' he called to her, over his shoulder.

'No worries. Honestly, I'm fine.' The dreamy note in her voice hinted at inner satisfaction. 'Take as long as you need,' she called back.

Left alone while Drakon retreated to his glass office, Lucy wandered around, feeling deeply content. It felt almost as if she were *floating*. As if she were walking on air. She didn't even mind her new husband shoehorning in a little work, despite his avowed intention to put business on the back burner during their honeymoon. Who cared if he'd succumbed to a call from his busy empire when this brief time together had exceeded all her expectations? When their interactions as a couple had filled her with the tentative hope that they shared a basic compatibility which could grow, if they nurtured it—and that maybe this marriage could become more than she'd ever dreamed it could be.

She texted Sofia, who informed her that Xander had discovered the use of his hands while they'd been away and had been trying to grab the soft toys attached to the sides of his cot.

Lucy texted back.

Sounds very advanced for a seven-weeker! Can't wait to see you both tomorrow. X

And it was true. She couldn't. Funny how you could bond with a tiny baby, even when you didn't realise it was happening. Even when it wasn't your baby. Couldn't they become a *real* family, she wondered hungrily, even if it was a somewhat unconventional family?

She glanced up as Drakon returned, his

expression slightly preoccupied as he walked into the room. 'Is everything okay?' she questioned.

'Mmm?' He glanced across the room at her as if he had only just noticed she was there. 'I'm going to have to deal with a conference call a little later.'

'Oh? Must you?'

'Yes, I must,' he said smoothly. 'I'm afraid it can't be helped.'

It was disappointing. Of course it was—and part of her wanted to ask him to put whatever or whoever it was on hold, so they could enjoy every last second on the island. But Lucy was made of stronger stuff than that. She might have sometimes resented the military life in which she'd grown up, but being an army brat had taught her how to be strong and resilient. She needed to remind herself why Drakon had married her. Mostly because he wanted a mother substitute, but hand in hand with that went his own need for a supportive wife. She had to look on anything else as a bonus, rather than with any sense of entitlement.

'That's okay,' she said. 'I might do some packing so we aren't rushing in the morning.'

And that was how Lucy spent the last evening of her honeymoon. She took a long bath and washed all the sea water out of her hair. Then she packed her case and started reading a previously unopened novel she'd brought with her.

And though it was difficult to empathise with a woman who found herself marooned in a snowy cottage on Christmas Eve with a brooding stranger—*why on earth had she set out for the cottage when the weather forecast had been so atrocious?*—Lucy gave it her best shot.

At least Drakon made it down in time for dinner but he ate more perfunctorily than with any obvious signs of enjoyment and refused Spiro's home-made baklava, which made the chef go into a slight sulk. Only at bedtime did things settle into an agreeably familiar pattern, when her new husband took her to bed. He pulled the duvet over them like a private snowy tent and began to kiss her, and all the faint frustrations of the evening were forgotten. He made love to her very quickly, as if he were seeking some sort of release—but Lucy wasn't going to analyse that either. She just revelled in the elation which pulsed through her veins afterwards. Because this was bliss. Being in Drakon's arms was like finding her own tiny piece of heaven. Through heavy-lidded eyes she studied his profile, his skin silvered by the moonlight which flooded in from the windows, his indifferent expression giving nothing away.

'Did you sort all your business out?' she questioned.

He frowned. 'Are you really interested in talking about that right now?'

Was that censure which underpinned the hint of mockery in his voice? 'I thought you might want me to show some interest,' she said, a little defensively.

'Well, I don't. At least, not in that. Only in this.'

Lucy's head fell back against the pillow as he gave a featherlight flick of his tongue against her nipple and she squirmed when he licked some more and his hand crept down between her thighs. And although warm desire flooded through her, it was followed by a feeling of frustration which had nothing to do with the physical. Because this was a familiar pattern with Drakon, she recognised. He used his physicality to distract her from subjects he had no desire to pursue. And it worked. Every time. That was the magical yet ultimately infuriating thing about her husband. That he had the power to manipulate her. To use sex to quieten or console her— and there didn't seem to be a thing she could do about it.

They left the island at noon the following day and arrived in London just as dusk was falling and the Christmas lights in the city were starting to glow in the fading light. Inside the lobby of the luxury apartment block shone a glittering tree she'd barely noticed before the wedding—and this evening it seemed to symbolise a faded air of festivity which echoed her own increasingly flat mood. In the elevator she badly wanted Drakon to kiss her but he was busy looking at his phone and Lucy knew she needed to ruthlessly prune any romantic fantasies instead of allowing them to grow. They'd had a great honeymoon. So what? That didn't change anything, did it? That didn't mean he'd suddenly started to care for her, did it? Yet she had started to care for him even more than she'd done before. That was the truth of it.

Be careful, Lucy, she thought. *Be very careful.*

The elevator doors slid open and she walked straight into the apartment, where a smiling Sofia was waiting with Xander in her arms. The baby was dressed in a green sleepsuit covered with red-nosed reindeers and Lucy felt a welling up of something hard in her chest which took her breath away as she cradled the infant. He was so tiny and helpless and…she'd missed him, she realised with a wrench. Had Drakon missed him too? she wondered, turning her head to speak to her husband.

'Drakon? Look. See how he's…' But Lucy realised she was talking to an empty space. That Drakon had slipped from the room without a word and, from the fading sound of his conversation, it appeared he was already on the phone to somebody.

She tried not to let it bother her as she played with the baby. She bathed him and fed him and sang a crooning little song she remembered from those long hours of night duty when she'd worked in the neonatal unit at St Jude's hospital. She gave Sofia the evening off and, once Xander was asleep, Lucy changed into a dress she'd never worn before. Before she'd met Drakon, she would never have dared. Silky scarlet jersey clung to her hips and the slashing V neckline gave an uncharacteristic glimpse of shadowed cleavage. Spiky-heeled black shoes with scarlet soles completed the outfit and she styled her hair into a fashionably messy topknot which the Granchester hairdresser had showed her how to do.

Zena had prepared a meal which she'd left for them and Lucy was just lighting tall candles in the dining room, when Drakon walked into the room. The top two buttons of his shirt were undone and she could see the faint darkness of chest hair, which arrowed downward in a beguiling path. He hadn't changed since they'd arrived back from Prasinisos, she realised, narrowing her eyes. He must have been on the phone all this time. He was looking around the room, taking in the holly-strewn centrepiece with tall silver candles which adorned the table and the bottle of champagne which protruded from an ice bucket.

'This all looks very…festive,' he observed, with the air of a man who had just been told that his dentist was about to make an unscheduled visit.

'Doesn't it?' Lucy said brightly. 'Zena must have gone to a lot of trouble and it's still… well, it's still Christmas.'

He turned his attention to her outfit. 'Is that why you're dressed like the personification of seasonal sex in your Santa-red dress?' he questioned huskily. 'Because you want me to unwrap you?'

Lucy swallowed as her nipples tightened in time to his slow scrutiny. 'I don't see why not,' she whispered. 'We might no longer be on honeymoon, but that doesn't mean we can't still make love after dinner every night, if you want to, which I'm rather hoping you do.'

'Who knows what either of us will want? This is still all very new—to both of us.' He picked up the champagne bottle and began to tear the foil from its neck. 'Let's just take it one day at a time, shall we, Lucy?'

His voice was soft but entirely devoid of emotion, and as she looked into the unfathomable darkness of his eyes Lucy wondered whether he intended his words to sound more like a threat than a promise.

CHAPTER NINE

DRAKON SAT BACK in his chair and twisted the stem of his wine glass between his fingers as he studied his wife who was sitting opposite him in the large dining room of his Mayfair apartment. Candlelight flickered over the polished table and over the dark, coiled gloss of her hair. 'Did I mention that I need to go to Singapore tomorrow?' he questioned.

Lucy looked up from her bowl of Greek lemon chicken soup, her spoon suspended in mid-air. 'No, you didn't.' A frown criss-crossed her brow. 'Tomorrow? Just like that? Without any kind of warning?'

'That's business, Lucy.'

'It seems to be a very demanding business.' She hesitated. 'When you always seem to be working.'

He shrugged. 'Billion-dollar empires don't

just happen without someone putting in the legwork.'

'It would be nice…' her voice trailed off and, once again, she seemed to be picking her words carefully '…if you could spend a little more time with your son.'

Drakon felt a flicker of irritation because that felt almost like a criticism, and it was not in her remit to criticise him. But why not placate her when he was going away tomorrow, by wiping that look of uncertainty from her face? 'That will happen,' he said. 'When things are a little quieter.'

She looked unconvinced and maybe he couldn't blame her for that because, in truth, his heart was not engaged in fatherhood. He could see her hesitating, worrying her teeth into her bottom lip as if she was trying not to say something, but she said it all the same.

'Do you *have* to go, Drakon?'

She tried to keep the question casual but in this she failed because it was a refrain he'd heard from women countless times over the years and Drakon tensed—because didn't her words almost *justify* his intended trip? Didn't they reinforce what he suspected was her growing emotional dependence on him and make him aware of the subtle ways she was trying to steer him away from his work? But she had to understand that no way was he going to take his eye off the ball, because he'd seen what could happen if you did. He was still his own boss and a man who answered to nobody—not to his adopted baby and certainly not to his wife—and the sooner she realised that, the better.

Steeling his heart against the reproach in her eyes, he shrugged. 'I'm afraid I do,' he answered coolly. 'I don't know if I mentioned that we're trying to extend our oil refinery—'

Her voice sounded stiff. 'No, I don't believe you did. You don't exactly encourage me to keep up with what's going on in your empire, do you?'

Ignoring the underlying complaint in her question, he picked up a piece of home-made pitta bread. 'Amy hasn't been able to get anywhere with the government. She keeps coming up against opposition—she suspects it's because she's a woman—and I really do need to be there.'

'Of course you do.' But Lucy put her soup spoon back down on the plate, her appetite suddenly deserting her. Was that because, although Drakon was going through the motions of *sounding* apologetic, the anticipation in his voice suggested he really wanted to go off on a last-minute trip to the Far East? And wasn't the truth of it that he probably felt trapped in a marriage he'd never really wanted?

Because the honeymoon was over. At least, that was how it seemed to her. Within twenty-four hours of returning to London from Prasinisos, life had picked up a new routine and Lucy realised just how much time she was expected to spend on her own. Drakon had resumed what she was to discover were his habitual twelve-hour days at the office, leaving her at home with Xander, Sofia and the rest of his large contingent of staff.

She took to rising deliberately early in order to eat breakfast with her husband before he left for the office, knowing he wouldn't return until dinner time. Because what was the point of being married if you never got to see the man you'd married? At least when she was pouring strong coffee and offering him a croissant—which he would invariably refuse—she felt as if she was going through the motions of being a married woman. But only at night did she feel like a real wife, when Drakon undressed her and took her into his arms. When he made her cry out with disbelieving pleasure as his lips and fingers and tongue opened up her senses. Her breasts would grow full and aching—her nipples pebbling into tight little bullets as he grazed at them hungrily with his teeth. She opened her legs and took him deep into her body, his hard heat filling her and making her feel, well…complete. Was it crazy to admit that was the effect he had on her? Suddenly she could understand all those things she'd read about successful sex—as if some kind of transformational magic had taken place between two people.

Afterwards she would lie in his arms, her ear pressed close to his chest, listening to the dying thunder of his heart. Their legs would still be entwined and she could feel the sticky trickle of his seed on her thigh as she longed for him to say something—*anything*—which would make her understand just how he really felt about her. But there was nothing— which made her conclude that he felt nothing. Inevitably, he would fall asleep straight away, leaving Lucy lying there, her eyes adjusting to the mysterious shadows which seemed to be lurking in the corners of the vast room. Was this how it was going to be from now on, or was there a possibility that their incredible physical closeness might eventually lead to some kind of emotional bond?

The signs weren't promising. At times, she still felt like something he had acquired—in the way he might acquire a new yacht. One morning he presented her with a credit card—a shiny platinum affair which glowed against the starched white linen tablecloth, as he slid it across the table towards her.

'What's this?' she questioned blankly.

'Surely you can work that out for yourself, Lucy.'

'A credit card?'

'I thought you'd be pleased. You need your own money,' he added, in response to her blank stare.

'But how can it possibly be my money when I haven't earned it?'

It was a naïve question and maybe she deserved the answering elevation of his brows.

'You could work a million hours a week and never earn a fraction of what I do,' he said, his gentle tone not quite taking the sting out of his words. 'You shouldn't have to come to me every time you want to buy something. What if you want to get yourself a new car? Or redecorate the apartment? Put your own stamp on it. That kind of thing.'

Her own stamp. Lucy gritted an automatic smile as she poured him a cup of the strong black coffee he seemed unable to function without. His statement would have been funny if it hadn't been so sad. Because how could she possibly make her presence felt when her brilliant billionaire husband dominated everything and everyone around him? She had no desire to change a beautifully decorated home just for the sake of it—because that would be a terrible waste of money and that wasn't the way she had been brought up. But she was certainly going to have to find something to do with her days, other than help Sofia look after Xander.

Xander.

A lump rose in her throat. The child she was loving more with every day which passed. Was it knowing that he was going to be her *only* child which made her feelings for him so fierce and fundamental? Sometimes when Drakon was at the office she found herself staring down at the infant lying sleeping in his crib. The infant still largely ignored by his adoptive father—unless you counted the perfunctory kiss Drakon sometimes planted on his head if ever his return from the office managed to coincide with Xander being awake, which wasn't often.

Sometimes Lucy found herself wondering if he timed his arrival home deliberately, to make it so. If he was determined to keep his distance. Why, even on Sundays—Sofia's and the rest of the staff's day off—the workaholic tycoon didn't go out of his way to bond with his baby son, did he? He still managed to absent himself for long periods of time, going out for a sprint around Hyde Park and returning covered in spatters of mud with his black hair clinging in damp tendrils to his neck. Or holing himself up in his home office to read through long contracts with horribly small print.

True to his word, Drakon went to Singapore the very next day and was gone for two weeks. Two whole weeks with phone calls his only method of communication. He blamed their sporadic nature on the time difference between London and Singapore and maybe that was true. But to Lucy it felt as if they were a million miles apart, rather than six and a half thousand. All he seemed to want to talk about was how brilliantly the talks about extending the oil refinery were going. He even sent a photograph of him and Amy sitting in some plush restaurant in the famous Botanic Gardens of the city, having dinner with a load of government ministers. Lucy felt as if he were standing on the deck of a ship which was moving further and further away from her. And all she could wonder was whether this was how it was going to be from now on.

'So, when are you coming back?' she asked.

'Tomorrow lunchtime. I've asked for the plane to be ready at midnight.'

Lucy spent the day trying to contain her state of excited expectation, but at the appointed hour she heard her phone ringing, rather than the welcome click of Drakon's key in the lock.

'Where are you?' she said as his name flashed up on the screen.

'*Agape*, forgive me.' He paused. 'A last-minute meeting was scheduled with the trade and industry minister.'

'And you had to be there?'

'Yes, of course I did,' he said coolly. 'Do you have a problem with that?'

Too right she did, but Lucy held back from saying so because the sensible side of her knew she was being unreasonable, while instinct told her she was only going to make matters worse if she turned this into a battle.

Yet Drakon was worth fighting for, wasn't he? For Xander's sake mostly, but for hers too.

Because no matter how much she tried to tell herself it shouldn't be happening, her feelings towards the man she'd married were growing—feelings which had never been part of their marriage deal. Unstoppable emotions which had been nurtured during their brief honeymoon and taken on a life of their own. She tried blaming it on her lack of experience, convincing herself that a woman who'd reached the age of twenty-eight without ever having sex would be in danger of mistaking physical pleasure for something else. Something which felt uncomfortably like love. And she didn't want to love Drakon. The last thing she could afford to do was to waste her emotions on a man who'd told her right from the start that he didn't believe in love. Because that would be a self-destructive course and would detract from something she *could* do. Something positive and good—which was to strengthen the bond between father and son.

Because if Drakon wanted their marriage to endure, which was what he *said* he wanted—then he couldn't keep the baby at arm's length the whole time, as he'd been doing until now. She didn't think he was necessarily being unkind to Xander. It was just that he didn't know *how* to love him because he had no experience of parental love to fall back on. Maybe he had to learn to be a good father another way, and maybe she could help...

So just do *it,* Lucy thought to herself. *It's no good complaining about the state of your life if you don't do anything to try to improve it.*

She spun into action that same day, signing up for family membership at the local gym which she sometimes passed on her way to the park. Mayfair didn't run to budget gyms so the one she joined was eye-wateringly expensive, but it did have the benefit of a super-sized swimming pool. She tried it out a few times—in fact, her hair was still damp when Drakon arrived back from Singapore, his black eyes faintly bemused as he saw the drying locks of hair clouding around her shoulders.

'What's all this?' he questioned as she went into his arms to kiss him.

'I've joined a gym.'

'That's good,' he said absently as his phone began to trill in his pocket.

She made no further mention of it until the following Sunday morning, just as Drakon replaced his empty coffee cup and told her he was going to read through a new contract in his study, but Lucy shook her head, feeling her heart pounding nervously in her chest.

'I'd much rather you didn't.'

There was a split-second pause. 'I'm sorry?'

'Not today, Drakon. I wonder…' she licked her lips '…would you mind coming swimming with me and Xander instead?'

'Swimming?' he demanded. 'Don't be ridiculous. At his age?'

'They can start lessons as early as four weeks,' she informed him calmly. 'In fact, he's had a couple at the new gym already but they've got a class this morning and it would be nice to have some company.' She sucked in a deep breath. 'I think you might enjoy it. And before you trot out all the reasons why that's not possible—can I just ask what's the point of being one of the world's most successful men if you take less time off than the average factory worker?'

Drakon met her resolute expression and felt a flicker of mild irritation at the fact that she was so openly defying him. Yet he couldn't fault her logic, no matter how much he'd like to be able to. In fact, there was little about his new wife he could fault—and hadn't that been the biggest revelation of all? She was…

He studied her.

She was *surprising*. She was like the first soft shimmering of spring after the harshness of winter. Like a welcome sea breeze which whispered over your skin on the hottest day of the year. Her skills as a mother had never been in question because Drakon had known exactly what he *didn't* want from someone taking on that particular role. His mouth hardened. He'd wanted someone as unlike his own mother as possible—without her brittle exclusion of her own children, and her all-encompassing absorption in her philandering husband, and her preoccupation with her own appearance. He'd wanted someone soft and caring and honest and true. Someone with a heart and someone with a conscience—and Lucy had ticked all those boxes, and more.

He swallowed. Much more.

He hadn't been expecting her to keep surprising him as a lover, nor imagined he would find it difficult to drag himself away from the seductive sanctuary of her arms each morning. Sometimes he would even find himself glancing at his watch at the end of a working day and itch to get away, but he forced himself to work as late as he'd always done, because independence was key to his success. Wasn't that one of the reasons why his Singaporean trip had provided such a welcome relief and the space he needed? Because no way was he ever going to rely on another human being and open himself up to pain.

Yet Lucy wasn't asking for the world, was she? She wasn't demanding emotional reassurance, or expecting him to bolster her unrealistic dreams about marriage. She simply wanted him to accompany her while she took the baby swimming. Not the biggest ask in the world.

'What time do you want to leave?' he growled.

'In about an hour.'

'I have a couple of calls I need to make first.'

'Of course you do,' she said, with a smile which somehow niggled him.

The gym was only a short walk away, reached through an oasis of a garden square which was new to him, but then, it was a long time since he'd taken a walk in London just for the sake of it. Feeling like a man who had just emerged from a long sleep, Drakon heard the unmistakable sounds of birdsong coming from the bare branches of a tree, before peering down at a carpet of snowy white flowers whose white tips were pushing their way through the grass.

'Snowdrops,' said Lucy as she followed the direction of his gaze.

'I know they're snowdrops,' he snapped.

He was slightly disconcerted to discover mixed changing rooms at the upmarket gym—he hadn't been in *any* kind of changing room since uni—and by the way Lucy thrust a pair of impossibly tiny armbands at him.

'Could you put these on Xander?'

He looked at them with a frown. 'Can't you do it?'

'Well, I *can*, of course—but I thought you might like to.'

What could he say in response? That he had no desire to do so? That the thought of touching the baby filled him with dread because he was so impossibly tiny? Especially as a nearby blonde was openly listening into their conversation, her eyes devouring him in a predatory way he hadn't come across in a while. Was that because he never really looked at other women any more, other than to compare them unfavourably to Lucy? He shot the blonde a glance before disdainfully averting his gaze. She was practically falling out of some skimpy bikini and he thought how much sexier his wife looked, clad in a sleek one-piece which hugged her toned curves.

He turned back to the task in hand and stared down at the tiny baby who was now cradled in the crook of his arm. It was a nerve-racking experience to slide on the arm-bands and he wanted to lash out at Lucy for making him do it, when he looked up and met the soft understanding shining from her blue eyes.

'You're doing just fine,' she said softly. 'Babies are stronger than they look and all dads feel funny at first. I've seen men the size of mountains looking completely lost when confronted with a newborn. You just need to do it more often. You know what they say. Practice makes perfect.'

But Drakon could hear his heart pounding. Pounding in a way he didn't recognise. Xander was wearing a hooded little towel which made him look like a miniature caped crusader, but nothing could detract from his vulnerability, despite the fact that he was over three months old now. Drakon stared into black eyes framed by impossibly long lashes. He had his father's eyes. Niko's eyes, he realised with a wrench. But they were *his* eyes too, for hadn't he and his twin brother been identical, sharing almost the same DNA? He stared down again at his adopted son and something inside him turned over and started to melt.

And that was how it started. Insidiously at first, but with gathering force—like the fierce Meltemi wind which blew through his homeland every summer—Drakon began an emotional connection with the child he had adopted.

He tried to deny it. To convince himself his life wouldn't change in any way because he didn't want it to change. He would play the part of husband and father, yes. That had always been part of the deal. But he would play it from a suitable distance, for that was how he operated. He was there to support Lucy in her role of mother, because that was her primary role. At times he'd started to wonder whether she truly understood and accepted the boundaries within their relationship, then something happened which made it clear he was going to have to spell it out for her.

The episode in question occurred when he

was returning from a day trip of meetings in France and found his limousine waiting for him at the airfield. Unusually, the chauffeur remained in the driving seat and Drakon opened the rear door himself, to discover Lucy sitting on the back seat waiting for him—a vision in a silky dress which matched her eyes and suede high-heeled shoes in exactly the same colour.

'Hi,' she said.

'Hi,' he said, his eyes narrowing as some unknown fear clouded his heart. Something to do with Xander, perhaps? 'Is something wrong?' he demanded.

'No, nothing's wrong. I just thought it would be fun to come and meet you for a change.' She crossed one pale, stockinged leg over the other and tilted him a smile he'd never seen her use before. It was a slightly nervous smile but also kind of...*predatory*.

His senses were on instant alert as he got in beside her, noting the tense atmosphere inside the tinted interior of the car. He could see that she'd floated up the soundproofed and darkened screen which separated them from his chauffeur, so they were in a private world of their own. As the powerful vehicle pulled away she leaned forward to kiss him, guiding his hand up her skirt to illustrate the fact that she wasn't wearing panties. Before too long she had unzipped him and was straddling him, easing herself slowly down onto his rigid length and riding him as if they were in some kind of erotic rodeo. He felt compromised and manipulated but his desire for her was so intense that he had no choice other than to submit to her sexy ministrations. Even when inside her he tried to hold back—to make her wait for what he knew she wanted—but suddenly his seed was pumping out and he was moaning softly against her mouth.

It was undoubtedly the most stimulating homecoming he'd ever experienced—possibly because it was so unexpected. It was hard to believe this was the same blushing virgin he'd seduced on his Mediterranean island, and that disturbed him almost as much as this sudden reversal of control. He'd chosen her for her suitability and purity. Didn't she realise that he had chosen her because he had wanted a mother for his son? If he'd wanted a vamp, he would have married one.

'So what was all that about?' he demanded, once he'd got his breath back.

She paused in the act of smoothing down her rucked skirt before looking up, and he was caught in the teasing crossfire of her bluebell eyes. 'You didn't like it?'

He didn't respond to the feigned innocence in her voice. 'I didn't say that. I just wondered if there was any particular reason for such a mind-blowing homecoming and whether this is something I should expect every time I take a flight in future?'

Something in the repressive tone of his voice sent a shiver down Lucy's spine. He was looking at her with a stony expression in his black eyes, which somehow contradicted his passionate response, and she felt a worm of worry wriggling away inside her. Should she tell him the truth? Should she confess she'd been concerned he might find too much domesticity and fatherhood stultifying and she wanted to reassure him that she intended to remain as exciting a lover as possible? But that might let too much light into her occasionally paranoid thoughts and make what had just happened seem almost...*predictable*. Surely it would be better to allow a little mystique to prevail. To keep her gorgeous husband on his toes and ensure he'd never get bored and want to walk away from her, because that was something she couldn't bear to contemplate.

Still a relative novice to the game-playing of romance, she flicked him a smile. 'You'll just have to wait and see, won't you?'

'I guess.'

But her attempt to engage him again fell disappointingly flat for he picked up his brief-case and began rifling through it, effectively dismissing her. Quickly Lucy looked out of the window, terrified her gaze would betray her feelings, though he wasn't actually looking at her. But if he was…

She swallowed. If he was then mightn't he recognise that she was falling in love with her Greek husband, even though she knew there was no way he would ever return those feelings? Even though he now seemed to be in a strange kind of mood after she'd plucked up enough courage to travel to the airfield to seduce him. She never knew what was going on inside his head, because he rarely told her. Sometimes she felt as if they were growing further apart rather than closer, despite their cohabitation. Yet when he relaxed enough to let his guard slip…didn't she adore the man who existed behind the brittle exterior he'd formed to protect himself? The man who'd suffered such a loveless childhood, which meant he kept all his emotions locked away.

And didn't she cherish a hope that his feelings for his son were growing—and would continue to grow if she could help facilitate that?

But it was hard to communicate with someone who was increasingly absent and Lucy's growing sense of insecurity was fuelled by Drakon jetting off again. This time he was travelling to Indonesia with Amy and communication filtered down into the usual snatched phone calls, squeezed in around the time difference. Lucy kept herself busy with Xander and that was always a pleasure. A growing pleasure. With every day which passed the baby was growing more and more aware and when she went in to him each morning, she was rewarded with the sunniest of smiles. Sometimes he nuzzled his silky little head against her neck, and Lucy felt a pure joy which was almost *painful* in its perfection. He was just gorgeous. The most gorgeous little baby in the world.

She had just put Xander to bed, sung him a small medley of lullabies and was standing beside the crib watching him when she heard an almost imperceptible sound by the door and glanced up to see Drakon standing silhouetted there. Lucy's heart leapt with instinctive longing but when he made no move to join her, she crept from the nursery to find him waiting for her in the corridor. After days of absence, his powerful body looked especially muscular and virile, though the expression on his dark face seemed much sterner than usual.

'How long have you been standing there?' she whispered.

'Long enough.'

'I wasn't expecting you back until Friday.'

'I know. I tried to ring a short while ago, but you didn't pick up.'

'I was bathing Xander.'

'So I see.' He smiled then. 'Your hair is damp.'

Self-consciously, she patted the dishevelled strands. 'I'd better go and tidy up. Don't you want…to say goodnight to Xander?'

He shook his head. 'I don't want to risk waking him. I'll see him in the morning.' There was a pause. 'Would you like to go out for dinner tonight, Lucy? Just the two of us. I thought we could try that new Italian restaurant in Knightsbridge.'

'I'd love to,' she said, a little breathlessly. 'I'll go and get changed.'

'Why don't you wear that green dress you

had on the other night?' he suggested carelessly, his words fading away as he walked towards one of the dressing rooms.

Lucy hurried away to get ready, wondering if she was just imagining that Drakon's mood seemed…*different* tonight. Had something happened during his business trip to Indonesia? Had he met a woman and realised how constrained his life was by marriage to someone he was only with because it happened to be *convenient*? Was that why he had asked her to wear her admittedly on trend but least sexy dress, with its high ruffled neck and knee-length skirt?

She was silent in the car on the way to the restaurant but Drakon seemed too preoccupied with his own thoughts to notice. And it wasn't until they were seated at a table at the far end of the discreetly lit eatery in Knightsbridge, with two Bellini cocktails sitting in front of them, that she plucked up courage enough to ask him. Because hadn't he seemed more distant than usual, ever since that time when she'd surprised him at the airport in the back of the car? Moistening her lips with the tip of her tongue, she stared into the dark gleam of his eyes.

'Is something wrong, Drakon?'

He paused for long enough to magnify all her unspoken fears. Long enough for her heart to begin pounding painfully hard in her chest. But what he said next made Lucy's heart pound even louder.

CHAPTER TEN

'I WANT US to have another baby, Lucy.'

Lucy's fingers dug into the linen tablecloth as she struggled for words which wouldn't seem to come. 'What…what did you say?' she croaked.

He leaned forward. Close enough for her to reach out and touch his gorgeous face and on some instinctive level Lucy was tempted to do just that, knowing in her heart that in a few minutes' time such a move would inevitably repulse him. Because wasn't this the moment she'd been waiting for? The moment she had been secretly dreading?

'Another baby,' he repeated. 'A child of our own.'

'A child of our own,' she echoed dully.

'*Neh.*' His black eyes glittered. 'It makes sense.'

'Does it?'

He didn't seem to register the wobble in her voice and Lucy was grateful that her hair was successfully concealing the prickles of sweat which were beading her brow.

He nodded. 'Of course it does. Perfect sense.'

'B-because?'

He sucked in a deep breath before the words came out in a rush, as if he'd prepared them before saying them. 'Because Xander needs a brother or a sister. I don't want him growing up in a world occupied solely by adults. I want him to have someone to play with. Someone to keep him company. Someone who is there for him, fighting his corner. I want us to be a real family. To give him the brothers and sisters he needs, which might help erase the terrible start he endured at the beginning of his young life.' He paused, and his black eyes had suddenly grown very intense. 'And you are such a good mother that I think you need a child of your own to love and care for, as you have loved and cared for little Xander. Don't you, Lucy?' His mouth quirked into a reflective smile. 'Something more worthwhile to keep you busy, rather than having to put on silk stockings to come and meet me at the airport.'

Lucy stared at him in dismay, and not just because he was making her sound like some kind of amateur hooker. Because this was the moment she'd dreaded. The moment she'd prayed would never come. But in the long run, mightn't it all be for the best? Couldn't admitting the bitter truth she'd nursed for so long provide some sort of catharsis for them all? Drakon had said he wanted a real family and she wanted that too. Couldn't she show him that what they already had could be enough, if they were prepared to work at it? With an effort she composed herself, acutely aware of the fact that they were in a public place.

'Perhaps we should order first,' she said.

He narrowed his eyes. 'Some men might be offended by your preoccupation with dinner,' he observed, with a flash of mockery. 'Are you so hungry that you can't wait a moment longer or do you just want to make me suffer by making me wait for your answer?'

It was more the fact that she could see the waiter hovering in the background and Lucy didn't want him coming over and disturbing them when she was in the middle of her story. The story she wished above all else she didn't have to tell. Just as she wished that Drakon had worded his proposal with more affection and that he wanted more children for reasons which had to do with love, rather than expediency. But it was pointless wishing for the impossible. She knew that better than anyone. With cold dread, she cast her eye over the menu and chose something which would take ages to prepare and then attempted to speak as if she actually cared about it. 'Why don't we have the chateaubriand, to share?'

'If that's what you want.'

If only he knew that the only thing she wanted could never be hers. Lucy spoke quickly to the waiter and, once the order had been given, clasped her hands together as if praying for a courage she wasn't sure she possessed.

'Drakon. There's something…' Her voice trembled. 'Something I haven't told you.'

His body tensed—as if her tone was warning him that what she was about to say wasn't just some undiscovered quirk of character. 'Oh?'

She sucked in a deep breath but the air which made its way to her lungs was scorching her airways. 'I can't give Xander the brothers and sisters you want for him,' she husked, 'because I'm…'

Go on. Say it. Say those two painful words which you've never quite been able to get your head around.

'I'm…infertile.'

There was total silence as he sat back in his seat and Lucy searched his face for some kind of reaction. But there was none. His enigmatic features were as unreadable as they'd ever been, and somehow that felt much worse than open pain, or anger.

'Have you known about this for long?'

The conversational tone of his voice gave Lucy the hope she needed and she nodded. 'I found out while I was nursing. It's one of the reasons which made me leave midwifery. I found it…' She swallowed as she tried to convey some of the pain she'd felt—not just the physical pain of endometriosis, but the emotional pain of knowing her womb was always going to be empty. 'I found it increasingly hard to be around pregnant women and babies. Every day when I went into work, I was reminded of what I could never have.' She searched his expression but still she could pick up nothing from his hard-featured stillness. 'It's one of the reasons I never really had any boyfriends before you, because most of the time I only felt like a shell of a woman.'

And now the cold words which began to fall like stones from his lips gave her a clue as to what he was feeling.

'But you didn't think it was pertinent to tell me all this before we were married?'

'I meant to. But we didn't really know each other back then, did we? It's not the kind of thing you just casually drop into the conversation with a virtual stranger.' She licked her lips. 'And it didn't seem relevant, because you said you didn't ever want children of your own.'

'But things change, Lucy,' he ground out. 'We're both intelligent enough to realise that. People change their minds all the time. I would like to have been given the choice instead of having it taken away from me, without my knowledge.'

Lucy shook her head, but it didn't change the fact that her throat felt as if someone were pressing their fingers against it, making it almost impossible to breathe. But she needed to breathe. To try to explain how it had been. How it had felt. 'A couple of times I intended to tell you—but the right time never seemed to come up,' she said. 'The preparations for the wedding were so intense and all-consuming that I never found the opportunity to start a conversation about it.'

'You could have made the time,' he said repressively.

Her head was hurting and so was her heart. She could sense that he didn't understand and she wanted to make him understand. 'Did you ever see that film about Queen Elizabeth I—the one which won all the awards?' she questioned suddenly.

'What?' he demanded, his dark look of accusation momentarily morphing into one of perplexity.

'The English Queen was almost completely bald, and she hid her baldness beneath a lot of elaborate wigs,' she rushed on. 'But they said that anybody who had seen her in her true state could never look at her in quite the same way again. That she remained permanently ugly and scarred in the mind's eye of the beholder. And that's how *I* felt, Drakon. I didn't want you to look at me as less than a woman. As some barren creature only to be pitied. I wanted you to continue to desire me and want me.'

He gave a short and bitter laugh. 'So you lied to me?'

'I did *not* lie!' she protested. 'The subject never came up.'

'Oh, but you did. It was a lie by omission—and deep down you know that, Lucy.'

She stared at him, unable to deny his bitter allegation.

'It was a lie by omission,' he repeated with quiet force, his face a blur of rage. 'In fact, I don't think I've ever met a woman who *doesn't* lie. It seems to be stamped into their very DNA. I learnt it first from my own mother, almost as soon as I'd left the cradle, and I've been having it reinforced on a regular basis ever since.'

Lucy heard a note of *triumph* which edged the cynicism in his voice as their meal was brought to the table, and she watched in excruciatingly tense silence as the meat was carved into neat slices and heaped onto their plates.

'I guess in a way this has made you happy?' she ventured, once the waiter had gone.

'Happy?' he echoed. 'Are you out of your mind?'

'Not at all. This must be a self-fulfilling prophecy for you,' she said slowly. 'You don't like women and you don't trust them—you never have. And I've just given you yet another reason to hate us as a sex.' She sucked in a deep breath. 'The only thing I can say to you, Drakon, is that I'm sorry. And if I could have the time back, I would do it differently.' She could hear her voice starting to wobble. 'Except that then you might never have wanted me and I would never have become your wife and learned to love you as I do.'

'Love?' he queried disdainfully. 'You think I want your tainted love, Lucy? That I want to spend the rest of my life with a liar?'

Lucy recognised that their marriage was hanging precariously in the balance. That a delicate line as fine as a spider's web was all that lay between happiness and loneliness. One clumsy move and it would all be lost. Yet surely what they had discovered together was worth fighting for. Fighting with every single breath in her body. 'But we're all capable of lies by omission. Of fashioning reality to look like something quite different,' she pointed out quietly. 'Even you, Drakon.'

'What the hell are you talking about?'

'I'm talking about your close friendship with Amy. So close that even your godfather told me he thought the two of you would get married and so did everyone else. And before you remind me that Amy's gay—surely that's all part of it. She hasn't come out, for whatever reason—so it probably suits her very well to have people speculate on the true nature of her relationship with her business partner.' She took a sip of her cocktail and felt the champagne and peach juice foam against the dry interior of her mouth.

'That's different,' he snapped.

'Is it?' she questioned quietly. 'Oh, Drakon.' Her voice was filled with a deep sadness which she couldn't seem to hold back. 'Can't you ever forgive me? Can't we just put all this behind us and start over—now that everything's out in the open?'

But she got her answer instantly as he rose to his feet, towering over her and the table, his muscular shadow seeming to swallow her whole.

'I'll tell you exactly what's going to happen now,' he said quietly. 'I'm going to pay the bill and leave. And then I'm going outside to catch a cab. You can take the car.'

'I don't want your damned car!'

'Really? Then how are you proposing to get back to Milton tonight?'

'To Milton?' she repeated blankly, blinking her eyes at him in sudden confusion. 'You mean, back to my cottage?'

'Of course that's what I mean! Where else did you think you'd be spending the night,

Lucy? Do you really think I want you in my home in the light of what I've just learned?'

'Drakon…' Lucy felt as if she had fallen down a deep well only to discover there were no footholds to allow her to get back up again. She had expected his censure, yes, and his condemnation, too. Deep down she'd felt as if she deserved both those things. But surely not such an instant and outright rejection, which felt so final and so *permanent*.

'What did you *think* was going to happen after this astonishing revelation, Lucy?' he demanded cruelly. 'That we would just go back to Mayfair and pretend nothing had happened? That we would make love and carry on as normal?'

She shook her head as a pair of dark eyes and a silky head swam into her mind. 'But what about Xander? What's going to happen to our son?'

'Xander has a nanny—and a father,' he said coldly. 'We don't need you, Lucy. Perhaps we never did. I will arrange to have your stuff sent to the cottage—'

'Please don't bother. Keep it!' she said furiously. 'I won't be able to wear those kinds of clothes in Milton, anyway!'

'That's entirely your decision. Oh, and I

don't think I have any further use for this, do you?' he added contemptuously. She saw him twist his gold wedding band from his finger before letting it fall with a tiny clatter onto an unused side plate and fixing her with a final withering look. 'Obviously I will make sure your settlement is generous, provided you agree to a swift, no-claim divorce. I don't think there's anything else, do you? Other than to say goodbye.'

He turned and made his way through the restaurant, oblivious to the curious eyes which followed him, and Lucy wondered if she would be able to manage that same degree of insouciance. But most of all she wondered just how long she would be able to keep the hot flood of tears at bay.

CHAPTER ELEVEN

Don't forget Xander's check-up appointment at the clinic tomorrow. Sofia already knows but thought you might like to accompany them. L

DRAKON STARED AT the text message from his estranged wife which had just appeared on his phone and his brow creased in a frown. It wasn't the first he had received—all to do with the welfare of his son, he noted, and all signed off with Lucy's initial and not a single endearment.

Initially, he'd been surprised that she'd bothered contacting him, given the unceremonious way in which he had dumped her at the Italian restaurant. But wasn't that a mark of Lucy's soft and caring nature—that she wouldn't allow hurt pride to stand in the way of her concern for the baby she had mothered so beautifully? Another stab of the pain pierced relentlessly at his heart. The same damned pain which had been plaguing him since her departure. Fury and denial rose up inside him in a hot and potent mix. He kept telling himself it wasn't *her* he missed—it was her presence as Xander's mother which was making him feel so remorselessly uncomfortable.

And an inner voice mocked him every time that thought came into his head, because deep down he suspected it wasn't true. For a man so enamoured of the truth, wasn't he falling short of his own high standards? Because hadn't Lucy taught him how to relax around his son, so that now he felt completely confident whenever he cradled little Xander in his arms? Yet it hadn't always been that way. A lump rose in his throat and his heart began to pound. Before Lucy had come into their lives, the realisation that he must adopt his orphaned nephew had lain heavy on his heart. It had been a task he had been prepared to undertake—but Drakon's attitude had been reluctant. Not any more.

He stared down at the sleeping infant and his heart clenched. These days he embraced fatherhood with a sense of immense satisfaction and with something else, too. Something he'd never thought he'd feel towards Niko's baby—and that something was love.

Restlessly, he left the nursery and moved aimlessly through the Mayfair apartment which had felt so vast and so empty since his wife had moved out. He missed her in his bed at night—and the hard, physical ache which greeted him each morning bore testimony to that.

Just as he missed talking to her over breakfast and dinner and swimming with her in the Greek sea on a winter day when surely no sane person would have swum.

He had the services of the best nanny in the world and the wherewithal to find another any time he wished. He had an address book practically overflowing with women who would be eager to provide him with whatever consolation he required.

He drew himself up short, reminding himself that he didn't *need* consolation—because that would imply that he was grieving for something and he wasn't.

Really, he wasn't.

Of course she missed him. That was only to be expected. But it was *Xander* she missed, Lucy convinced herself fiercely. She certainly didn't miss his pig-headed father. And of course it was weird being back in her tiny riverside cottage and waking up alone every morning, without the warm and muscular body of Drakon stirring beside her in more ways than one. But she would get over it. She had to. And all things passed eventually—some just took longer than others.

At least she'd got her job back. She had telephoned Caroline and had a brief and uncomfortable conversation. Her mentor and employer had diplomatically agreed not to quiz her about the reasons for the end of her brief marriage and Lucy had gone back to work as a waitress. The jobs were busy and distracting—which was probably a good thing—and she tried her best to pin on her brightest smile, hoping it would conceal the pain of missing the family life she'd so nearly become a part of.

One night she put on her pale green uniform and went to work at a large house outside the town, handing out canapés to the guests of a local landowner whose daughter had just got engaged. The whole affair seemed destined to mock Lucy, from the moment she was diverted to enter the house via the back door and told to tidy up her hair, to someone impatiently dismissing her and her tray, as if she were a large fly who had just landed on a piece of sushi and started laying eggs. She'd forgotten how patronising the rich could be, when you were in a position of domestic servitude. The newly engaged woman was flashing her massive and rather vulgar ring and, stupidly, Lucy found herself thinking about the discreet ink-spot sapphire which was tucked away at home with Drakon's discarded wedding band, which she had snatched up before leaving the restaurant, and wondering whether she ought to send both back to her estranged husband.

The moon was high in the sky by the time she left the party and, although transport home was included, Lucy had no desire to sit on a steamy and overcrowded minibus, especially as she was always the last one to be dropped off. Despite the ever-present drizzle, she set off to walk along the familiar roads and lanes, pausing briefly by a small footbridge, to watch the dark gleam of the water as it flowed beneath her. Because the river never changed, she thought gloomily. It had been the same all through her life and would be the same once she was dead and gone.

An unfamiliar sense of melancholy washed

over her as she brushed past a low-hanging branch of wet leaves on the final approach to her cottage and tiny droplets of water showered over her. And then she nearly jumped out of her skin as a large figure loomed out of the darkness, her instinctive fear quickly replaced by an intense feeling of longing as she identified the late-night intruder.

Drakon.

Drakon Konstantinou, in all his towering and muscular beauty. Her heart twisted with pain and regret, but indignation was a far healthier reaction and that was the one she clung onto. 'What the hell do you think you're doing, jumping out of the shadows like that?' she demanded. 'You gave me a fright.'

'And what are you doing walking back alone at this time of night?' he returned furiously. 'Anything could have happened to you!'

'I can't think of any fate worse than my former husband turning up unannounced like this!' she retorted. 'What are you doing here, Drakon—have you come to gloat?'

Despite the darkness of the night, Drakon could see the fury spitting from his wife's eyes and his heart sank. Because this wasn't what he had planned. He'd thought she'd be home and he'd be able to talk his way into the cosy comfort of her small cottage within minutes. But the place had been in darkness and he'd been walking up and down this damned riverbank for hours, his tortured mind conjuring up pictures of where she might be, especially since her phone had been switched to silent and she hadn't bothered to return any of the calls he'd been making all evening.

Yet could he blame her for being so angry?

No, he could not.

Rarely in his life had he been forced to admit that someone else had the higher moral ground, but he did so now, repeating the same words he'd used when he'd turned up on this very same spot a few months back, asking her to marry him.

'Can I come in?'

'No, you can't. Contact me through my lawyer.'

He frowned. 'Have you got a lawyer?'

'Not yet. But I will. At least I suppose I will—isn't that what people do when they're going through a divorce?'

'I don't know, Lucy, because I've never been married before and I don't want a divorce.'

'Well, I do! I can't think of anything worse than—' She stopped abruptly, as if his words had only just sunk in, and eyed him suspiciously. 'What do you mean, you don't want a divorce?'

'There's no qualifier to that statement,' he said drily. 'I just don't.'

'Well, I do.'

He sucked in a deep breath as he read the defiance on her shadowed face. 'We can't have this conversation on the doorstep.'

'We seem to be managing perfectly well, so far.'

'Open the door and let's go inside, Lucy,' he said gently. 'Your hair's all wet.'

Lucy wanted to shout at him. To tell him not to adopt that silky tone which made her think of all the times he'd cradled her after they'd made love and made her feel so cherished and protected and wanted. Because all that stuff had been an illusion. It had withered and died at the first test, hadn't it?

Yet she recognised it would be immature to send him away when he had come all this way to see her. They needed to deal with this situation like adults. He probably wanted her to promise not to give her side of the story to the press—as if she would dream of hanging out all her heartache for the world to see. And besides... She glanced nervously at the look of determination which was making his jutting jaw look so formidable. She swallowed. He didn't look anything like a man who would accept being turned away.

'Oh, very well,' she said crossly. 'But this had better not take long.'

She made him wait while she lit a couple of lamps and put a match to the fire because the temperature in the room was positively arctic. Then she took off her comfy black work shoes and shot him an acid look as she lined them up next to the others in the hallway. 'I'm assuming you won't be spiriting away any of my shoes this time?' she questioned sarcastically.

But he didn't rise to the bait. Instead he walked over to the window and stared outside, his head bent and shoulders suddenly hunched, like a worn-out fist-fighter on the brink of defeat who was about to make one last stab at victory. 'I just want to say that I'm sorry, Lucy,' he said, and when he turned round Lucy was shocked by the ravaged expression she could read on his rugged features.

'It doesn't matter,' she said woodenly.

'Oh, but it does. It matters a lot. It matters more than anything else in the world that you realise how bitterly I regret the things I said to you that night.'

She shook her head, because hadn't her nurse training taught her always to see the other person's point of view? 'It doesn't,' she repeated, as generously as she could. 'We all say things we sometimes regret when we're angry. Or even when we're not angry. It's okay, Drakon. Honestly.'

'No, it's not okay,' he flared. 'It's anything but okay. Stop trying to be kind and reasonable, even though those are the very qualities which drew me to you in the first place.'

'Stop talking like that and just tell me why you're here, Drakon,' she demanded, her voice trembling with anger, because she didn't need to know these things. In fact, weren't they making the situation even worse?

'I'm here because I miss you, Lucy,' he bit out. 'I miss you more than words can ever say and in every way—physically, mentally and emotionally. And Xander misses you, too.' He shook his head. 'I can't believe I didn't even let you say goodbye to him.'

'But Xander has a nanny,' Lucy put in fiercely, because it wasn't fair for him to do this to her. To put her heart through the wringer all over again, only to leave her high and dry. 'As you told me on the night we parted. Just as you told me you couldn't tolerate a woman who had lied to you. And as for not saying goodbye to a baby of that age—what difference would it have made? Xander is too young to have realised what was going on and it would only have upset and confused the baby and Sofia.'

'But that wasn't why I did it,' he persisted. 'Why I wouldn't allow you to go to him.'

'No. I realise that. You did it to punish me because I had failed to live up to the image you'd created of me as your ideal woman.' She drew in a deep breath. 'Because that's the truth of it, isn't it, Drakon? You'd put me on a pedestal and that's where I was expected to stay. The nurse. The virgin. The mother. And you didn't like it when I blurred those roles, did you? When your good girl became a good-time girl and seduced you in the back of the limousine, you could hardly hide your dismay. You couldn't bear to accept that I had flaws, just like everyone else—or that I was a real person with real needs. Maybe if you hadn't been so intent on perfection, I might have had the courage to tell you I was infertile before. But I didn't want to risk you not marrying me,' she admitted huskily, because what did she have to lose now? 'I had an opportunity to do just that when we first discussed it, over lunch in the Granchester that day, when you presented me with my engagement ring.'

'But you didn't?' he questioned slowly.

'No, I didn't. You didn't ask why I didn't want children of my own and I was glad you hadn't, because in that moment I was living the dream and I didn't want to wake up from it. And like I said, we didn't really know each other—there was no expectation that we would ever care for each other—so why would I confide something so intensely personal?'

There was silence for a moment and when eventually he spoke, his voice was very low. 'What if I were to tell you again that I'm sorry for what I did and that I care very much? What if I were to tell you that my life has been empty without you and that I love you and want to spend the rest of my life with you and our son?'

Lucy couldn't prevent the surge of hope which flooded into her chest, but she quashed it and forced herself to ask the question which still hung between them, like a dark spectre. 'But you want more children, Drakon!' she declared, her voice shaking. 'That hasn't changed. You want more children and I can't give them to you.'

'I wanted more children with you,' he corrected sombrely. 'And if that isn't possible, then I will count my blessings and be content with the family I've already got. All I'm asking is for another chance, Lucy. To show you that I mean what I say. To love you in the way that you deserve to be loved.'

Lucy stared at him as those two words resonated more than any others. *Another chance.* How could she deny him that, even if she wanted to? Because how many people would give everything they owned for one more chance? Her brother would have liked the chance to have dodged that stray sniper's bullet—and if that had happened, her mother would never have faded away, like the blowsy roses which grew in the walled garden at Milton school.

She swallowed, knowing that this was the biggest and most important decision she'd ever had to make. If she accepted Drakon's offer, she would be taking a risk and she had never been a natural risk-taker. But what was the alternative? To turn him away and say goodbye? Yes, she might get hurt if she stayed with him—that was a very real possibility in every single relationship—but wasn't she being given the opportunity to spend the rest of her life with the only man she had ever loved? And wouldn't the hurt of turning him away transcend any other pain she'd ever known?

Because Lucy had glimpsed a world without Drakon in it and it was a bleak one. And maybe this place in which they now found themselves was the best place of all. One where all the barriers and fears with which they had surrounded themselves had crumbled away and all that was left were two people who loved each other and wanted to be together. She clasped her hands together as if in prayer and looked at him with all the tenderness she had never dared show before.

'Yes, Drakon,' she said softly. 'Yes, to everything you ask of me. Because I love you, too. I love the man I see beneath the hard layer you present to the world—and I'd like the world to see more of him.'

He nodded as he took a step towards her. 'Just know one thing, Lucy.' His voice was shaking as he pulled her into his arms and buried his face against her hair and she could feel his powerful body trembling. 'That I won't ever let you down. Not again.'

But Lucy knew that already, in the only place which mattered.

She knew it in her heart.

EPILOGUE

'YOU'RE NOT COLD?'

'Cold?' Lucy smiled up at Drakon. His arm was protectively clasped around her shoulders and she thought how handsome he looked in his dark dinner suit and black bow tie. 'Not at all. Mainly because I'm wearing thermal knickers.'

'Are you joking?'

'Of course I'm joking, darling. Do you really think I would have passed over all that deliciously decadent lingerie you bought me for Christmas in favour of a pair of sensible pants? And besides…' She snuck a glance at the jewel-studded wristwatch she'd also found nestling at the bottom of her stocking a week earlier. A delicate watch with ink-spot sapphires he'd had made specially. 'It's not long to wait until the fireworks.'

Her husband's black eyes gleamed as he

studied her. 'Do you know how much I love you, Lucy Konstantinou?' he questioned softly.

'I think I've got a good idea. Just so long as you understand that the feeling is completely mutual, my darling. *S'agapo*.'

Noting Drakon's nod of contentment at her increasingly confident use of Greek, Lucy took the opportunity to look at the lavishly dressed guests who were milling around, drinking champagne beneath the fairy lights on the roof terrace of the Granchester Hotel as they waited for midnight.

'People seem to be having a good time,' she whispered. 'Don't you think?'

'Mmm,' he said, more concerned with dipping his head to brush his lips over the fall of her hair. 'The best time in the world, but of course—the moment I'm most looking forward to is when the fireworks are over and I can take you along to the penthouse suite to continue our own, very private party.'

'I'm looking forward to it, too,' said Lucy. 'Though I'm still not quite sure why we're staying the night here, when we only live down the road in Mayfair and have a car at our disposal.'

'I thought you might enjoy sleeping in the

same bed we occupied on the first night of our honeymoon.' His mouth quirked. 'Or not sleeping, as the case may be.'

Lucy gave a contented sigh. 'You are a very romantic man, Drakon Konstantinou—as well as being an exceedingly sexy one.'

'I do my best. Because I gather that's what you like.' He whispered a fingertip over her waist. 'Am I right, *agape mou*?'

'Irrefutably,' she purred.

It was New Year's Eve and Drakon had thrown the party to end all parties to celebrate the discovery of a new oil field, which was being mooted as the biggest find in almost a century. And although Lucy sometimes mused that he really didn't need to earn any more money, the philanthropic arm of his empire had benefited in so many ways that she couldn't really complain. Her husband had taken over the entire hotel and the evening was—apparently—the hottest New Year ticket in town. Movers and shakers had flown in from pretty much every country in the world, as well as Hollywood actors and international sports stars, whose arrival was thrilling the growing crowds who had gathered outside behind the roped-off barriers.

Everyone who'd been at their wedding

was here. Caro and her husband, as well as Lucy's two waitress friends, Judii and Jade. Patti and Tom were enjoying their first outing since the birth of their second child. And Amy was there too, with her not-so-new partner and proclaimed love of her life. Lucy smiled. When she and Drakon had decided to give their marriage another go, he had arranged a meeting with Amy. Gently, he'd explained to his business partner that the smokescreen of their close working relationship must necessarily end, because he intended travelling a lot less in future and spending more time with his family. Perhaps his words had galvanised her into action, for Amy had taken Michelle to meet her parents and told them she was in love. And in the end, perhaps her parents had recognised that their daughter's happiness was more important than a prejudice which they simply had to learn to let go of.

Lucy sighed as she stared up at a clear and starlit sky, which boded well for the eagerly awaited fireworks. What a long time ago their wedding seemed now, and how the years seemed to have flown by in the time it took to blink your eye. Three whole years—and back then she'd been so scared. A trembling mass of nerves in her too-fancy dress as she'd walked down the aisle towards a man she'd never stopped wanting. She'd never for a moment imagined she'd get love and devotion from someone who made no secret of having a heart of stone. But Drakon's heart wasn't made of stone, she'd realised. These days she would describe it as a heart of gold—for he had learnt to show his love, not just for her, but for their darling little Xander, who flourished with each day which passed.

'Something is different about you,' Drakon said, his velvety voice breaking into her thoughts.

Lucy turned her attention away from the star-spangled sky to study the ruggedly handsome face of her husband. 'What do you mean, *different*?'

He shrugged. 'You've been…thoughtful all day,' he said slowly. 'And your face has a kind of radiance about it which I've never seen before.'

How perceptive he was, Lucy thought, and savoured the moment before telling him what she still couldn't quite believe herself. 'I'm pregnant, my darling,' she said softly. 'I'm having your baby, Drakon.'

He stared at her without comprehension

and it was several dazed moments before he could speak. 'But you said—'

'That I had endometriosis and because of that I was infertile, yes. That's what I was told. So when I started getting symptoms of pregnancy, I thought it must be something else. But when I saw the doctor this morning, she confirmed what I hardly dared dream. She told me that miracles do happen, and this is ours, Drakon—our very own miracle.'

Drakon felt a lump rise in his throat and the hot spring of tears at the backs of his eyes as he put his arms around her and held her tightly against his beating heart. Not for the first time, he wondered what he had done to deserve a wife like Lucy. A woman who had been prepared to take on an orphaned baby and to love the helpless tot without condition, just as she loved him. She had forgiven her sometimes irascible husband his many transgressions and taught him the things in life which were truly important, and the most important of these was love.

'I discovered that myself on the day I met you again, my love,' he said gruffly. 'Although it took me a long time to realise it.'

She pulled back from him. 'Realise what?'

'That miracles really do come true. Some-

times they are right in front of your eyes…
you just have to let your vision clear for long
enough to see them properly.'

'Oh, Drakon,' she said shakily.

The first chime of Big Ben rang out and
the guests began counting down the seconds
towards midnight. Trumpets sounded and
streamers were popped and people started
to sing as the final chime faded away. But as
one year merged seamlessly into the next and
a kaleidoscope of fireworks exploded on the
London skyline, nothing came close to the
burst of joy in Drakon's heart as he held Lucy
tightly in his arms, and kissed her.

* * * * *